The

Dressmaker's Cottage

De-ann Black

Paperback edition published 2021

The Dressmaker's Cottage

ISBN: 9798460074310

Also by De-ann Black (Romance, Action/Thrillers & Children's books). See her Amazon Author page or website for further details about her books, screenplays, illustrations, art and fabric designs.
www.De-annBlack.com

Romance:

Embroidery Cottage
The Dressmaker's Cottage
The Sewing Shop
Heather Park
The Tea Shop by the Sea
The Bookshop by the Seaside
The Sewing Bee
The Quilting Bee
Snow Bells Wedding
Snow Bells Christmas
Summer Sewing Bee
The Chocolatier's Cottage
Christmas Cake Chateau
The Beemaster's Cottage
The Sewing Bee By The Sea
The Flower Hunter's Cottage

The Christmas Knitting Bee
The Sewing Bee & Afternoon Tea
The Vintage Sewing & Knitting Bee
Shed In The City
The Bakery By The Seaside
Champagne Chic Lemonade Money
The Christmas Chocolatier
The Christmas Tea Shop & Bakery
The Vintage Tea Dress Shop In Summer
Oops! I'm The Paparazzi
The Bitch-Proof Suit

Action/Thrillers:

Agency Agenda
Love Him Forever.
Someone Worse.

Electric Shadows.
The Strife Of Riley.
Shadows Of Murder.

Colouring books:

Summer Garden. Spring Garden. Autumn Garden. Sea Dream.
Festive Christmas. Christmas Garden. Flower Bee. Wild Garden.
Faerie Garden Spring. Flower Hunter. Stargazer Space. Bee Garden.

Embroidery books:

Floral Garden Embroidery Patterns
Floral Spring Embroidery Patterns
Christmas & Winter Embroidery Patterns
Floral Nature Embroidery Designs
Scottish Garden Embroidery Designs

Contents

CHAPTER ONE

A Hot Summer Day

The dressmaker's cottage was situated deep in the forest above the beautiful Scottish coast. Summer sunshine filtered through the trees, highlighting the garden's flowers that arched across the old–fashioned trellis, edged the lawn and entwined themselves along the walls of the traditional two–storey cottage. Colourful climbing flowers decorated the cottage, and everything from delphiniums to cornflowers created a lovely blue hue amid the brightly coloured mesembryanthemums and other flowers. The warm air was filled with a heady floral fragrance and the distant scent of the sea.

Bees and butterflies fluttered through the air, disappearing into the lush greenery where the garden merged with the surrounding forest. The cottage belonged to the past, and had a vintage quality and magical atmosphere, especially on hot days in the heart of the summer when it looked like a rich and colourful watercolour painting from a bygone era.

Judith, the dressmaker's assistant, opened the patio doors wide at the back of the cottage, filling the living room with sunlight and the warmth of the midday sun. The fragrance of the flowers wafted in, mingling with the delicious aroma of home baking. A Victoria sponge cake with brambles and fresh whipped cream sat in a chilled area of the kitchen, baked that morning by Judith, along with fruit scones and a chocolate cake topped with a smooth, shiny layer of ganache.

Tea pots and vintage style cups and saucers with silver spoons were all ready for their visitor. A table was set with a lilac linen tablecloth, embroidered along the edges with a heliotrope and bellflower motif design, and a cake stand waited to be filled with the cakes and scones. Dainty sandwiches with cucumber, Scottish cheese and plum and tomato relish were prepared and set aside in the chilled area along with the cakes. It was a warm day, and as the midday sun rose to its height, it became even hotter.

'Emmie's late.' Judith sounded concerned. In her fifties, sturdy, with salt and pepper curls, she'd worked for many years as the

1

dressmaker's assistant. She wore a floral skirt and a pale lemon blouse. She'd made them herself at the local sewing bee, but she wasn't an expert when it came to sewing. Knitting was her thing, especially tea cosies, and most cottage owners in the area had at least one of Judith's personalised cosies. From bumblebee cosies for the beemaster's cottage, and a chocolate confection for the chocolatier's cottage, to a floral design for the flower hunter's cottage, Judith excelled at creating a theme to match each owner's interests. All given as gifts. 'I hope she hasn't changed her mind. I was looking forward to seeing those vintage dresses.'

'She'll be here.' The dressmaker's pale blue eyes showed no concern. Of retirement age, with a beautiful face and porcelain skin, she wore a lovely sky blue vintage style, drop–waist dress that suited her slender build. Her elegant blonde chignon was pinned with a classic pearl barrette.

This was enough for Judith to be totally reassured. 'Great. Will I start getting the tea set up?'

'Yes, she'll be here soon.'

Thimble, the dressmaker's black cat, glanced at them with vivid green eyes, then padded out of the room into the garden, jumped over the hedge, and disappeared into the greenery.

'Phew!' Emmie sighed, opening all the windows of her little white car in the hope of encouraging a breeze to blow in. Anyone doubting that Scotland could enjoy a heatwave with the best of them needed to come here in the height of summer. The day was a scorcher.

And so too was the half naked man she'd driven past five times. Or was it six? Trying not to look at him distracted from her maths.

Half naked...the words lingered in her thoughts as she tried to reword them. He wasn't exactly naked, just sort of not wearing a shirt, or vest or anything to cover his smooth, toned, hot bod torso. Those shoulders of his would need a good lathering of cream to cool them from the heat of the sun they were exposed to. Not that he was exposing anything particularly embarrassing. He looked cool, in his own way, unperturbed by the heat, stripped to the waist and wearing low–slung jeans that clung to his long legs and lean hips. She'd seen men like him in advertisements and films, but never sighted one for real.

She smiled to herself, sounding like a bird spotter, her heart fluttering that she'd seen her first stripped down version of a light brown haired, lithe, leanly muscled Adonis working in his cottage garden. It was his cottage, surely. He didn't look like anyone's gardener. Though she supposed it was hard to tell from the scant information gleaned from his clothes, or lack of, what type of man he was. She was thirty and he seemed similar in age. But there was something about him...

He'd seen her and pretended he hadn't noticed her driving by, circling around the road past his picturesque cottage repeatedly like a moth to the flame. It wasn't deliberate. Her sat nav was on the blink, and although she was following the directions given to her by the dressmaker, it felt like she was chasing her own tail. And speaking of tails — there was that black cat again, sitting on a fence, green eyes watching her with curiosity.

She drove past the man in his cottage garden again, then pulled up further along under a canopy of trees where it was slightly cooler to reread the scribbled map. Yes, she'd taken the right turn on the left, driven past a beehive, one of the main markers, and then...seemed to keep bloomin' ending up ogling Mr. Hot Bod. His eyes were blue, stunning aquamarine no doubt, like the sea glistening in the distance far below the hills, because even at this distance she could see him surreptitiously glancing blue daggers at her, and probably sighing — *what is that woman up to?*

Hunter sighed heavily. *What is that young woman up to?* If she drove past his cottage one more time he'd be forced to do something about her. She was very attractive, and he wasn't averse to talking to a lovely young lady, but she was deliberately pretending not to notice him. An independent type he surmised. Stubborn. Her car number plates showed she was from Edinburgh. A city girl. Yep. He sensed the trouble brewing.

She'd disappeared under a canopy of trees. Hopefully she'd found wherever she was heading for and wouldn't...

Uh–oh! Here she comes again.

He put his garden shears down on the lawn and walked over to her.

Emmie pretended not to see him. If she kept driving, and took the wrong route, rather than the one specified on the map, perhaps she'd find her way. But she had to slow down as the road narrowed.

Oh, no. Here he comes...

Her heart started thundering in her chest, and on a scorching day like this the last thing she needed to cool her down was the sight of his bare, smooth, golden chest approaching and being highlighted in the rearview mirror.

He swept his hand casually through his thick, sun–lightened brown hair, a gesture that made the butterflies in her stomach flutter uncontrollably. This was ridiculous, she scolded herself. She didn't get affected by men like this so easily. Then again, she hadn't come face to face with one as luscious as him. Or maybe she'd been out too long in the midday sun and was hallucinating slightly.

'Are you lost?' His deep voice poured in through the driver's side window, causing her to look right into his aqua blue eyes as he leaned down to talk to her. Enviable dark lashes emphasised their beautiful colour and intensity. The breadth of his shoulders filled the window from all angles, and wow! This man had angles to die for.

His low–slung jeans emphasised the muscles at the sides of his torso. Those muscles that she'd never had a name for, like she'd seen on sculptures of men with perfect builds, whatever those side muscles were called. A distraction. That description would do for now. Especially as they were at eye level as he stood beside her window.

She shook her silky, golden brown hair from around her shoulders, wishing she could control her blushes. Hopefully he'd blame the heat of the day for her rosy cheeks and flushed complexion. She wore a summery floral print tea dress, but even wearing a cool dress like this felt too hot.

She tapped the map that showed a route into the forest. 'I'm sort of not lost, but somehow I keep not finding where I should be going.'

He pressed his firm, highly kissable lips together, attempting and then failing to keep his comment to himself. 'That's the definition of being lost.'

She supposed this was true, but no way was she conceding that point. Oh, no. Mr. Confidence and all aglow with manliness and...stop it! She took a steadying breath and forced herself to ignore

4

his handsome looks and regain some semblance of her dignity. Okay, so she was lost, and she should admit that, but having had a horrible run of rotten bad luck with ex–boyfriends and male bosses that made her feel like a dimwit, she'd become a bit defensive over some things. A few things. Actually, a whole load of things. But hopefully a short break in the Highlands would calm her senses and let her settle back down to her normal nature of being fine with the world, even when it was working against her on all levels.

'Where are you going?' he asked, trying to keep his voice calm, sensing she was the stubborn type and not inclined to admit that she was lost, and in need of assistance, especially his assistance. He was aware he'd taken his shirt off while doing the garden, but on a day like this, why not? Normally, no one would've seen him, or only in passing, once, not several times like she had, while defiantly trying to appear like she was well capable of navigating the route up to the forest. If she had trouble finding her way around here, she'd no chance once she entered the forest road.

'The dressmaker's cottage.' She indicated the location on the makeshift map.

'Ah!' he said, sounding as if all the pieces of the puzzle had slotted into place at once. His tone also indicated that there was a problem with this.

'What? Am I on the wrong road?' she asked when he wasn't quick enough to explain.

'No, you're on the right road, but...' he stood up, put his hands on his hips, emphasising his lean waist and flat, taut stomach. 'The dressmaker's cottage has a reputation. It's tricky to find. People can only go there if specially invited by the dressmaker herself.'

'She has invited me.' Emmie thumbed to the suitcases in the back seat. 'I've brought vintage dresses that once belonged to her. She wants to see them, and has invited me to have tea with her.'

She'd felt the need to explain herself and then wished she hadn't. It was none of his business.

He stepped back and looked around and sighed again. 'You'll need someone to take you there.'

'I'm not letting a half naked strange man into my car, thank you very much,' she was quick to tell him.

Half naked? He tried to stifle a smile, but his luscious lips curved up into a smirk.

'I wasn't proposing to get into your car, Miss,' he assured her, now leaning near the window again, all blue eyes and white teeth, causing her heart to squeeze just gazing at him.

Jeez–oh, he was a looker. And he was looking at her. He was clearly not amused. Or only on a smirking level. She'd done that thing she often did and instantly ruffled a man's feathers before she'd had a chance to let him see that she wasn't perpetually thrawn or awkward.

He started to walk away to his cottage, saying over his shoulder. 'I'll lead the way. You follow in your car.'

She assumed he was going to get into his car, though perhaps the sleek, dark sports car wasn't his. Tucked at the side of the cottage, she'd glimpsed it on passing.

Hunter threw on his sky blue T–shirt that he'd hung from the cherry tree, lifted his bicycle over the flowering hedge, taking a shortcut out of the garden, and cycled up to her car. 'The road is twisty–turny, so take it easy. Peep the horn if I'm going too fast for you to keep up.'

And off he went, making her hesitate for a moment, deciding if he was being straightforward or insinuating that she couldn't keep up with him and his bike. Taking a deep breath, she decided to follow him, at least to see if she could find her way into the forest.

She sighed again, feeling her temperature soar, not just from the heat of the sun streaming through the windows, but from the effect Hunter had on her. Now fully clothed, she couldn't blame his bare chest for causing her heart to flutter, but that blue top he was wearing fitted him so snug it emphasised his fit torso and muscled arms. She could see the strength of his broad shoulders as he held the handlebars, and the way his back tapered down to his waist and lean hips was a distraction.

She concentrated on the road, but wondered what a man like him was doing in a quaint cottage, which she now thought may not be his. The car wasn't his. He owned a bike, not a sports car, and yet...there was something about him that smacked of money, especially his attitude. Follow him indeed and peep if she couldn't keep up. That was a man confident in himself.

She drove behind him along a countryside road that narrowed as it led into the forest, leaving behind the glimpses of the sea far below on the stretch of coast where the water shimmered through the trees.

6

Cottages were scattered from the seashore upwards to the fields that rose towards the forest area. Gazing down, the sea glistened like liquid silver, and the boats in the small harbour and row of little shops added splashes of pastel colours to the beautiful but rugged seascape.

The road was indeed twisty–turny, and the trees shaded out more of the sunshine and provided archways leading deeper into the forest. The lush greenery appeared to glow with an extra intensity of moss and verdant hues, and the air was rich with the aroma of it, mixed with the last of the sea air that was then filtered out by the trees.

'Are you sure this is the right route?' Emmie called out to him as he led them into an area of the forest that looked like it belonged in a fairytale painting.

He braked, bringing his bike to a halt. 'It's a twisty road, but it'll take you to the dressmaker's cottage.'

Emmie checked her map. 'It seems to be the opposite direction to the route on the map.'

Hunter shrugged his broad shoulders. 'This is the way I know. I think your map may be wrong.'

Emmie put the piece of scribbled paper down on the passenger seat and allowed him to continue leading the way, though now he cycled right beside her driver's side window and proceeded to chat to her as he rode along. She glimpsed her pale grey eyes in the mirror. Thankfully her mascara hadn't run in the heat, but the creamy blush she wore that matched her lipstick was unnecessary as her natural blush was already overloaded. If he'd cycled on as he should've done instead of riding shotgun to chat, she'd have fanned herself with the map. Now she had to smile casually as if she wasn't feeling the heat — and not especially from the sun.

'What type of dresses are they?' He flicked a glance at the suitcases in the back of her car.

She doubted he was interested in the dresses and was using it as an excuse to chat. 'Vintage tea dresses. They're original designs stitched by the dressmaker herself.'

His blue eyes looked at her for a moment. 'Is it true what they say about her dresses?'

That they were beautiful, exclusive, expensive? She wondered what he meant.

7

Her hesitation made him elaborate. 'They say that the dressmaker is a bit fey, intuitive, and that she sews magic into her dresses. Not that I believe in fairytale stuff like that.'

'No, neither do I. But I don't know anything about the dressmaker or her dresses, apart from what I've read on her website. She designs exclusive fashions for movie stars, and has created the costumes for a couple of vintage era television series, and I think a film.'

He nodded. His light brown hair was now in the shade of the trees, but the sun lightened highlights still emphasised his thick, silky, well–cut locks. 'Yes, she's renowned for that. There was publicity about this in the press, about premieres she'd attended in London where the stars were dressed in her fashions.'

'Is fashion of interest to you?'

'No, I'm just...there's always folklore and imaginative tales in villages and communities like this, but people seem convinced that there's something special about the dressmaker.' So it made him wonder about the newcomer, and why she'd been invited to the dressmaker's cottage. 'I'm Hunter by the way.'

'Emmie.'

He smiled in at her, and then focussed on the road.

'I found the dresses online,' she felt the need to explain.

'Are you into vintage fashion?'

'Yes, I wanted to keep one of them, use the fabric from two and maybe upcycle the other three dresses.'

'That's a lot of dresses.'

'I bought them as a job lot. It didn't cost much. I trawled the sales online and saw these on offer. I think the seller didn't know their value, or wasn't fussed about it. So I got a real bargain.'

'What did you want the fabric for? Do you make...things?' He'd no idea what she would make.

'I enjoy sewing, updating old patterns, classic designs, reusing fabric rather than buying new all the time.'

'Make do and mend.' He'd heard the expression and had a vague idea what it was, but hoped it made him sound interested in their conversation.

'Yes,' she said brightly. 'I love make do and mend. And I use my embroidery to stitch over any marks or rips in the fabric.'

'Embroidery? You're an embroiderer?'

8

'I am. I design my own patterns.'

He looked curious. 'For a living?'

'Amongst other things. I have a little online business, and sometimes work for dress shops, making and altering dresses, including bridal wear.'

She thought she caught him glance at her ring finger, noting there was no wedding or engagement ring.

She was about to ask him what his occupation was when he indicated a niche in the forest. 'The dressmaker's cottage is over there.' He cycled ahead, putting on a spurt through the trees.

Emmie followed, and soon the cottage came into view. Trees surrounded the traditional cottage and flowers decorated the walls. Roses grew around the front door, and the garden was the loveliest she'd seen. The scent of the flowers and the forest blended into a heady fragrance, and she felt a sense of excitement build inside her as she parked her car in the driveway and stepped outside. It felt like stepping into another era, the past, as everything had a vintage air.

The curtains in one of the front windows twitched and a woman peered out for a moment before disappearing again.

Hunter dismounted and walked over to Emmie. 'I think you've been seen. So I'll leave you to enjoy your visit.'

It was only now that she realised how tall he was in comparison to her petite stature. She was about to thank him for his assistance when Judith came scurrying out, smiling and waving her to come in.

'We thought you'd got lost,' Judith said, beaming, clearly happy that Emmie had arrived.

'Hunter helped me navigate the route,' Emmie explained, and then lifted the two suitcases out of her car and started to lug them over to the cottage. The cases were old–fashioned and quite heavy.

Hunter put his bike aside. 'Let me carry those for you.'

He seemed adept at taking charge, and relieved her of the suitcases without any fuss.

'The kettle's on for tea,' Judith chirped, leading the way inside. 'I'm sure you could do with a cuppa and something to eat, Emmie. You too, Hunter.'

'No, I...eh...I was just—' he started to politely protest that he had no intention of coming in, but Judith cut–in.

'Come and have a cuppa before you go, Hunter. Or a cold drink. We've got homemade lemonade and ice cream if you're feeling hot.'

Emmie cast a glance at Hunter carrying the suitcases and trailing behind her and tried not to smile that he'd been inveigled in.

Blue eyes glared at Emmie, not wishing to upset Judith's polite invitation. There was an insistence in her tone that made him think that the easiest way to deal with the situation was to accept a quick cuppa and then be on his way. Though the thought of ice cream and lemonade appealed to him more than he wanted to admit.

Judith led them through to the living room where the dressmaker sat near the patio doors enjoying the fresh air. She smiled and stood up to welcome Emmie, and didn't seem surprised to see Hunter.

'Hunter showed Emmie how to get here,' Judith summarised. 'He's staying for a cuppa with us.'

The dressmaker smiled at him. 'Lovely to finally meet you, Hunter. And I'm so happy you're here, Emmie. I can't thank you enough for bringing the dresses personally.'

Emmie had offered to post them, but the dressmaker insisted she bring them in person in case they became lost in transit, or so she said. She really wanted to meet Emmie, and had a feeling that the ideal way to thank her was to offer her a short break staying in one of the cottages down the shore. The dressmaker owned the cottage, known locally as the strawberry jam cottage. The previous owner used to sell her own homemade strawberry jam that was popular with local customers.

'I was happy to bring them. And thank you for inviting me.' Emmie admired the shelves of fabric in the living room. 'This is an amazing room.' The floor to ceiling shelves were filled with beautiful fabric — everything from satin and chiffon to floral cotton prints. The walls were painted elegant pale blue–grey and enhanced the vibrant colours of the fabric. Everything was classic, as was the dressmaker herself.

Hunter put the suitcases down and glanced around. It was definitely a dressmaker's living room. But there was only one sewing machine, set up on a table near the patio doors. He'd expected there would be more than one machine, especially with all this fabric.

'The sewing room is through there,' the dressmaker told him. 'Would you be so kind as to put the cases in there for me?' She indicated to the room and smiled knowingly. 'I keep my main machine in here as I enjoy the view, but the other machines are set up in the sewing room.'

Hunter picked up the cases, happy to oblige, but wondered if she'd read his thoughts, or was used to explaining the layout of the cottage to visitors. He put the cases down, and noted that there were more shelves filled with fabric, jars of buttons, ribbons and trims, a cutting table that was set with pattern pieces, and various types of sewing machines.

Judith hurried through to the kitchen and came back with two glasses of iced lemonade. 'Here you go.' She handed one glass to Hunter as he joined them in the living room. And then gave the other to Emmie. 'Have a sip to cool you down, dear. It's such a hot day. You're looking a wee bitty flushed.'

Emmie smiled at Judith. If only she knew that Hunter was as responsible as the summer heat.

Judith busied herself preparing the tea, cakes and sandwiches.

But the dressmaker's blue eyes had a knowing look to them. She glanced at Emmie and at Hunter, and smiled to herself. She knew. Oh yes, she knew.

CHAPTER TWO

Secrets and Sewing

Hunter finished his glass of lemonade and made a bid to leave. 'I'm sure you're eager to see the dresses Emmie brought, so I'll leave you to it. Thank you for the lemonade.'

The dressmaker smiled. 'We're having tea first, so do stay and join us a little longer, Hunter.'

'Yes,' Judith chimed–in. 'The kettle's boiled and there's cake and sandwiches coming up.'

Without giving him room to outmanoeuvre them, Hunter was seated at the table and plied with tea and niceties. Though it didn't take much to encourage him to enjoy the delicious sandwiches and cake. He hadn't eaten anything since an early morning breakfast of a snatched slice of toast before attacking the garden that was badly needing tamed. He'd neglected it for three weeks, and in the summertime it had gone a bit on the wild side.

He sat opposite Emmie and noticed that her eyes were a beautiful pale grey that reflected her emotions so clearly in the sunlight streaming in through the patio doors. Her skin looked lovely and he wanted to touch it, run his hand gently down her cheek and feel the softness. He blinked the thought away and concentrated on enjoying the tea and company. He'd been on his own primarily for the past three weeks and it was nice to chat to these lovely ladies who were obviously happy to ply him with tea, sandwiches and cake.

'Help yourself to the cake, Hunter,' Judith encouraged him.

And so he did. 'Mmm, this cake is delicious,' he murmured, tasting the bramble and cream sponge.

'Judith baked the cakes this morning,' the dressmaker told him.

'I enjoy baking and knitting,' Judith added, and then summarised her position, working as the dressmaker's assistant, cooking, shopping, helping with the business side of things, but not actually a seamstress.

'So you don't make any of the dresses?' He seemed surprised at this.

'I can sew, and I made this outfit with help from the ladies at the local sewing bee, but the precision cutting...' She shook her head. 'I get too nervous about cutting the patterns from the beautiful fabrics. The dressmaker does the cutting most times, and she has an apprentice at the moment — Tiree.'

The dressmaker smiled. 'But Tiree is a little preoccupied with her romance with Tavion the flower grower. We're eagerly awaiting the date for their wedding. They've had to postpone their plans to accommodate Tavion's business, and Tiree is now helping him with his work, but they'll definitely get married. So she's not here as often. Though I want her to tend to her own life first.' She glanced at Emmie. 'But perhaps you'd like to assist me while you're here? I have several new dress patterns. Maybe you could help me with the fabric cutting.'

Emmie blinked. 'Yes, I'd love to. If you think I'm up to it.'

The dressmaker nodded assuredly. 'Oh, I think you are. You've worked for dress shops, making and altering clothes. I've had a lot more work to do recently and the cutting can be quite arduous, especially with the heavier fabrics.'

'I'd be happy to help with the cutting,' Emmie emphasised.

'Excellent,' said the dressmaker. 'And, as I've said, I truly appreciate you contacting me when you bought the dresses. I rarely see what happens to them once they leave here, especially my earlier designs.'

'When they arrived I could see that they were of a quality that was far more than I'd expected,' Emmie explained. 'When I checked for the designer, I saw...' she paused and smiled, wondering whether she should reveal this information in front of Hunter. Perhaps it was too private a snippet from the dressmaker's past and better left to discuss after he'd gone.

But the dressmaker had nothing to hide in that respect, and nodded for Emmie to continue, so she did.

'I saw tiny stitches, dots and dashes, as if something had been sewn in Morse code.'

This made Hunter's blue gaze spark with extra interest.

The dressmaker smiled, flicking a glance at him, as if she'd known this would be of special interest to a man like him.

'Morse code?' he murmured, frowning at Emmie and then looking at the dressmaker for clarification.

'It was very astute of you to notice that the stitches were indeed dots and dashes and not little running stitches and French knots along the inside of the neckline,' the dressmaker said to Emmie.

'I don't know Morse code,' Emmie was quick to say. 'But I looked it up online and realised that it was your name and where you lived — in the cottage.'

'I've lived here for many years, since I was a young girl, and my family moved here,' the dressmaker confirmed. 'I'm glad you found my website and contacted me. Anyone else might have kept the dresses, or tried to sell them for a profit, so it was very thoughtful of you to do this, Emmie.'

'I couldn't keep dresses like that, or cut into them like I'd intended. A trip here, away from the city, is thanks enough. It's nice to get a short holiday by the sea in a lovely cottage.'

'I'll show you the cottage later,' said Judith. 'You'll love it. It's so pretty.'

Hunter showed his interest again in the Morse code. 'So is it your practise to stitch your details in code?'

The dressmaker was happy to tell him. 'Life back then was filled with secrets, all sorts of secrets that I needed to keep about my wish to become a dressmaker. My father had other plans for my future, and they didn't involve stitching silly dresses as he referred to them.'

Emmie jumped in, sounding defensive. 'He must have seen your talent. Why wouldn't you be encouraged to become a dress designer?'

The dressmaker sighed. 'Things were different back then. My ambitions seemed frivolous, but later, when I started to establish my work, he understood the value in it. Though my parents passed before I'd ever made my mark as a dress designer.'

'Her parents wanted her to marry well and had high hopes of this happening,' Judith explained.

'But I didn't love any of the affluent men, the rich landowners and lairds, I was supposed to,' the dressmaker added. 'My heart belonged to someone unsuitable. A young man without wealth or prospects, as far as they were concerned. Though he did eventually do quite well for himself, or so I heard.'

This was the first time Emmie noticed a hint of sadness in the dressmaker's blue eyes. It was there and gone in a moment.

The dressmaker shrugged off her sadness. It seemed so long ago, though the memories and feelings remained clear. Her parents entrusted her upbringing more and more to her aunt in Falkirk and her grandmother in Dundee, hoping to put distance between her and the young man until he'd left the coastal village. He worked on the fishing boats down at the harbour, as did her father. And their plan worked. He found someone else to love, moved to the city, and she never saw him again. Her aunt and grandmother taught her dressmaking skills that she wouldn't otherwise have learned, and she pushed herself to achieve great designs in a bid to fight off her heartache. That too had worked, but at the cost of a broken heart. A heart that never really mended. But she always wanted to make her life in the cottage, at home, where she felt she belonged. 'So a past romance is partly responsible for where I am in life, here at the cottage, happy with my dressmaking, as much as it is with the dressmaking itself.'

'The paths we take in life lead to what we are, leaving behind what we might have been.' Hunter sounded as if he was quoting something from a book.

'Spoken like a true author, Hunter,' the dressmaker said to him.

He seemed slightly taken aback by her comment.

'How is your latest novel coming along?' the dressmaker asked him. 'I hear that you're staying in the cottage for the summer to work on your new book.'

Hunter smiled and toyed with his cake, shaking his head in dismay. 'No secrets in this village.'

'Very few,' the dressmaker conceded, smiling at him knowingly.

'You're an author?' Emmie's tone was filled with surprise. She'd never have taken him to be an author.

He nodded.

'A successful thriller writer,' Judith piped–up. 'I've read two of the latest books in your spy thriller series. Love them. When I start reading, I can't put them down. I've ordered the next one in the series from the bookshop down the shore.'

He smiled at Judith. 'Thank you, Judith. I'm pleased you enjoy them.' Though he seemed slightly embarrassed by the praise.

'I enjoy reading thrillers, especially ones like yours that have elements of romance in them,' Judith elaborated.

He thanked Judith and then brought the conversation back to the Morse code. 'How did you learn Morse code? If you don't mind telling me.'

'Ah, so it's going to end up in one of your books,' the dressmaker said with a wry grin.

Hunter shrugged his broad shoulders. 'I'm still working on the storyline of my new book. I've written a few chapters, and I'm hoping to get the bulk of it written while I'm staying here. But there's something missing. A great heroine. And an extra sense of mystery...intrigue.' He was clearly intrigued by the code written in the tea dresses all those years ago.

The dressmaker flicked a glance at Judith. A decision made. She'd tell Hunter the truth. 'My aunt was involved in working for a department of the government when she was a young woman.'

'Your aunt was a spy?' he asked.

'No, she was a code breaker. It was only for a short time, and when she got married, she stopped working for them and settled into a life as a seamstress. But she'd learned Morse code during her time working for the department. And there were things she knew, heard of, including coded messages stitched into clothing or knitted in garments. I don't know everything because she understandably kept that part of her life quite secret. It was in her past. But she taught me to stitch in code, and I stitched my details into the dresses I designed.' She paused. 'It seems so long ago, and I don't do that now. I was young and had secrets of my own.'

'Including keeping your ambitions to be a dressmaker a secret from your father?' said Emmie.

The dressmaker nodded, and Emmie sensed that there was a lot more to the dressmaker's past, perhaps involving work similar to her aunt, but that she'd no intention of revealing any more to them.

Hunter must have sensed that too because he didn't pry any further. If the dressmaker had been an agent, or worked in some sort of secret capacity when she was younger, he'd no intention of forcing her to tell him. He'd spoken to various people during the research for his books, people that were involved in the spying game, but no one made him feel as if he was transparent. It was as if the dressmaker could see right through his intentions, and perhaps she really was fey. If so, he wouldn't be able to wangle any secrets from her without her knowing exactly what he was up to.

16

Judith poured more tea for everyone.

Thimble padded in from the patio, looked at Hunter, and then settled down, stretching out in a band of sunlight on the floor near the dressmaker.

Emmie recognised the cat. 'He's your cat?'

'He is,' said the dressmaker. 'This is Thimble. Thimble the fifth to be exact.'

Emmie noticed the silver thimble dangling from the cat's collar. He was definitely the dressmaker's cat.

'Is your latest novel set in Scotland?' Judith asked Hunter. 'Or aren't you allowed to tell us until the book is published?'

'It's an international setting, like some of the other books in the series, but I want to include Scotland, maybe a seaside location like this one.' He shrugged. 'I haven't quite settled into the story yet. As I said, I feel there are elements missing, but that usually happens when I'm trying to write.'

'Are you living permanently in the cottage, or is it just while you're writing your novel?' Emmie asked him.

'My family own various properties, cottages, including the one I'm in. They live in the city. I have a house there too. But I find it's better to be far away from home, on my own, to think and write.'

'I must read one of your novels.' Emmie glanced at Judith. 'You mentioned that there's a bookshop down the shore.'

Judith nodded enthusiastically. 'Bea recently took it over. She's a lovely young woman. Ask her if she has the latest copy of Hunter's book. You don't need to have read any of the others to get into the story. It's brilliant. If you like exciting spy stories with a bit of romance, then you'll love it.'

'I do, so I'll definitely pop into the bookshop,' Emmie confirmed.

'I have a copy I'll give you,' Hunter offered.

'I don't mind buying it—'

'No,' he insisted. 'I'll hand a copy in to you. Are you staying here long?'

'Not long, just for a few days.'

The dressmaker smiled knowingly. 'I think you'll enjoy staying in the cottage down the shore.'

'Tiree lived there when she first arrived,' Judith told Emmie. 'She used to hold the local sewing bee in the cottage, but now the bee members meet at Ethel's cottage. The sewing bee is on tonight. You should pop along and meet everyone.'

'I'd like that,' Emmie confirmed. 'I've some embroidery I'm working on.' She hardly ever went anywhere without a sewing kit and her embroidery.

'Bring your embroidery with you,' said Judith. 'Come by at seven. Ethel lives in the wee blue cottage. You can't miss it. She's a knitter, like me, and spins her own hand dyed yarn. Do you knit or are you only into sewing?'

'I like to knit, though I'm no expert. I mainly sew. I especially like embroidery.'

'Yes, you're an embroidery pattern designer,' the dressmaker chimed–in. 'I had a peek at the patterns on your website. The floral designs and sea theme patterns are beautiful. Where did you train, or are you self taught?'

Emmie summarised her past. 'I was raised by my grandparents. They passed a few years ago.' She hesitated. She'd felt adrift ever since, on her own in the world, but sewing, especially embroidery work, had kept her going. 'My grandmother taught me to sew and I've always loved embroidery work and designing my own patterns.'

'Have you ever tried making dress patterns?' the dressmaker asked her.

'Yes, but I'm more experienced in alteration work,' said Emmie. 'I enjoy upcycling vintage clothes, especially dresses.'

As they started to chat about patterns and sewing, Hunter figured it was time for him to leave. He stood up. 'I'll let you ladies get on with your work, and I'll get back to my writing. Or rather, gardening.'

'Thank you again for joining us,' the dressmaker said, smiling at him.

The look he gave Emmie sent her senses alight, and a blush started to form on her cheeks.

He hesitated, wondering if he should ask her to have dinner with him, then decided not to be quite so bold. Besides, Emmie was only here for a few days, and he wasn't into light flirtations, especially as he liked her. He liked her the moment he saw her. But he let the chance go to invite her to have dinner.

Judith was about to accompany him out when there was a tinkle from the front doorbell. 'I wonder who that can be?' She glanced at the dressmaker. They weren't expecting anyone.

The dressmaker didn't seem perturbed. She nodded for Judith to see who it was.

Judith hurried through to answer it.

A tall, handsome, fit looking young man in his late twenties stood at the front door smiling. He thumbed to his car that was parked in the driveway. 'I have a delivery of fabric for you.'

'Oh yes,' Judith said, suddenly remembering that a delivery had been due, though it was always the postmaster himself that brought their deliveries to the house.

'The postmaster was up to his eyeballs in work,' the young man explained. 'I'm Calum. I offered to deliver the fabric while he dealt with the couriers and customers. I was coming up to the forest anyway.' He wore a black top and black sports trousers that emphasised his fit, lean, build. His arms and face bore a light golden tan from the summer sun.

Taking him at his word, Judith nodded for him to collect the fabric from his car and bring it in.

Calum lifted four large rolls of fabric that were carefully wrapped to protect the silk and satin, and carried them into the cottage.

Hunter was still in the living room, but was ready to leave. However, when he saw the handsome young man walk in, he hesitated, especially when the man's smile brightened when he noticed Emmie. They'd never met, but the spark of interest in her was clear from the man's reaction.

'The postmaster was busy,' Judith explained, 'so Calum brought our fabric order.'

'That's very helpful of you,' the dressmaker said to him.

'I was driving up to the forest to go for a run anyway,' Calum told them. 'This is lovely fabric,' he added, admiring the rolls of silk and satin in rich aquamarine and sea greens. The latter matched the colour of his eyes. His hair was dark, silky, ruffled, like a young man in his prime, clean and tidy, and yet still with an exuberant streak of wild youth in him. But his build was all man. A fair match for Hunter's physique, though Calum was packing more lean muscle

19

than average and bore a quicksilver element to his movements. Alert, sharp, and very, very fit.

'A run?' Hunter's inquisitive tone was edged with more than just curiosity, especially as he sensed Calum's instant attraction to Emmie. He understood this. He'd had a similar reaction, but Calum appeared to be without any sense of guile and didn't disguise his feelings.

'I'm in training,' Calum told him. 'I was going to run down the shore, but on a scorching day like this, I thought I'd run in the shade of the forest.' He picked his feet up deftly and mimicked how he'd run on the terrain. 'The roots of the trees will keep me sharp, challenge me, and it'll make a change from my regular runs.'

'What are you training for?' Emmie asked him. 'Are you a runner?' He looked like some sort of athlete. His black training shoes had a professional quality to them. She'd dated a man that was into sports training, but Calum seemed at the peak of fitness.

'No, I'm not a runner. I'm a boxer.' He didn't say this with any sense of achievement. He felt that being a boxer wasn't appealing. A brawler. A man who used his fists for a living. Some women liked the idea of it, but not the reality. He'd rarely lost a fight, and his face hadn't been badly cut or injured, but after a fight, he ached like crazy. No, the reality of it was an acquired taste when it came to romance. He looked at Hunter and had no idea who he was, but obviously he was a handsome man, not much older than him, but probably more the type that women liked. Too deep in his own thoughts, he suddenly pushed them aside, smiled and asked, 'Would you like me to put this up on the shelves for you?'

Judith was going to say no, but the dressmaker's reply was quicker. 'Yes, thank you, Calum. The silk goes up there beside the rolls of white chiffon, and the satin is stacked on the shelf higher up.'

Calum put the rolls where they belonged. 'There's more in the car. I'll bring them in.' And off he went.

'Would you like a glass of iced lemonade?' Judith called to him. 'And some ice cream?'

'Oh, great,' Calum called back, sounding as if he'd relish lemonade and ice cream.

Hunter wished he hadn't insisted on leaving, but it would look awkward if he hung around. 'I'll drop that book off to you,' he said to Emmie. Then he smiled at the dressmaker and allowed Judith to lead him out.

Hunter and Calum passed each other in the doorway. They almost clashed, but Hunter made way for Calum to go by with rolls of fabric hoisted on his broad shoulders, carrying them as if they were light as twigs.

If Calum sensed the edge of male rivalry, he made no mention or acknowledgment of it, and marched on into the living room. Like a handsome shadow, dressed all in black, he replaced the gap where Hunter had been.

Judith waved Hunter off as he got on his bike and headed away.

Hunter's heart felt heavy and he chided himself for the way he'd handled the whole situation. Calum was no doubt being plied with lemonade and ice cream. He shook his head at his own stupidity. If he could've thought of an excuse to head back to the dressmaker's cottage he'd have done it, but nothing sprang to mind, so he continued to cycle out of the forest and into the scorching hot day.

CHAPTER THREE

Vintage Tea Dresses

Calum explained that he'd lived in the forest earlier in the year. 'I had a fight lined up in January, and I came here to clear my thoughts and get ready for it.'

Judith gave him ice cream and lemonade. 'You were here in the winter?' She sounded surprised.

'For a few days,' he said, taking a sip of lemonade. 'The postmaster told my father that Bramble cottage was available. My father is my manager and trainer, and he's been friends with the postmaster since they were young boys. They trained at the same boxing club years ago. We live in the city, but they still keep in touch.'

A text message came through on Judith's phone. She checked it quickly and smiled. 'The postmaster has sent a message saying he sent Calum with the fabric delivery.'

'Tell him we received the fabric and Calum's been very helpful,' the dressmaker advised Judith.

Judith sent the reply and then they continued chatting to Calum.

'Bramble cottage sounds nice,' Emmie remarked.

'It was perfect. I'd love to buy it and settle down here rather than the city,' said Calum. 'The cottages down at the shore are great, but I prefer the forest. When I was here in the winter it looked and felt magical — everything covered with snow. Stepping out of Bramble cottage into snow, the air was so crisp and clear, and I never saw anyone or anything. I had it all to myself. It felt wonderful. I think it did me the power of good.'

Emmie sighed. 'It does sound perfect.'

'We have snow every winter,' said the dressmaker. 'White Christmases are guaranteed.'

'I'd come back again in a heartbeat, and maybe I will,' he said. 'I remember running past your cottage,' he told the dressmaker. 'That's how I knew I'd be able to find it when the postmaster gave me your fabric delivery.'

'We'd be sitting cosy inside by the fire,' the dressmaker told him. 'Though I do love the feel of the winter, opening the patio doors on a frosty morning. Everything in the garden sparkles with crystals, and sometimes I'll go for a walk in the forest in the snow. Not far, but it feels like a small adventure.'

'I know what you mean,' he said. 'There's a sense of excitement that you don't get in other seasons. I love the sound of my boots crunching through the snow when everything else is silent. Maybe winter is more my season, but I'm still enjoying the forest on hot summer days.'

'It must be wonderful sitting sewing in a cottage like this during the winter,' Emmie said to the dressmaker.

'It's truly magical. I hope you'll find time to come back and visit us again later in the year.'

Emmie nodded.

Calum frowned at Emmie. 'You don't live here?'

'No, this is my first visit. I'm from the city too.' Emmie went on to explain why she was here.

'My mother would appreciate the dresses,' he said, finishing his ice cream. 'She runs a dancing school, dance classes, and they put on shows and all love dressing up.'

'Are you a dancer too?' Judith asked him.

'I am. I can tango with the best of them, and I think the quick step helped with my footwork training for the boxing.' He indicated that he was light on his feet. 'I trained with my father in the boxing and went to the dance classes when I was a wee boy. If I'd been a better dancer I may not have pursued the boxing. But I had more aptitude for the fighting.' He shrugged. 'You have to go with what you're better at.'

'I've heard that boxing takes a lot of dedication,' said Emmie. She imagined the hits and bruises, the training, and fighting in a ring in front of an audience.

'Fighting is in my blood, but I don't know if it's in my heart,' he said.

Emmie nodded her understanding.

'With the boxing, I'm always training, always travelling, never settled.'

'It must be difficult,' Emmie acknowledged.

Calum smiled warmly at Emmie. 'I'm not always going to be a boxer. I trained as a chef and plan to open my own bar restaurant in a place like this. That would suit me fine. My father owns two restaurants and I trained with him, but I'd prefer to live here rather than the city. And settle down and get married.'

This remark made Emmie blush, especially as Calum looked right at her when he said it.

The dressmaker smiled knowingly. 'I'm sure you'll do well for yourself.'

'You sound very assured for a young man,' Judith remarked. 'Boxing must be hard, but if you're a chef a restaurant would be ideal for you.'

Calum nodded. 'With my father being into boxing, it was natural that I'd train too, but I seemed to have it in me to compete.'

'After you were here in the winter, did you do well in the competition?' Judith asked him.

He smiled and nodded. 'I did.'

'You won?' said Emmie.

He nodded again. There was no hint of ego in his manner.

The women smiled happily and congratulated him.

'My next fight is soon, and I'm glad I came here again to clear my thoughts and build up more stamina. Breathe in the sea air and the scent of the forest. I prefer training outdoors rather than the gym.'

He then asked the dressmaker about her work while he ate his ice cream.

'I've a lot of dresses to design and finish for another television series,' the dressmaker told him.

'You must be kept busy,' he said. 'But at least you have the forest and the sea to enjoy. A relaxing walk along the shore, that sort of thing.'

'The dressmaker doesn't go down to the shore these days,' Judith explained.

'Why not?' he asked.

His straightforward manner took them aback.

'It's complicated,' Judith said, hoping this would suffice.

Without guile, he frowned and tried to understand. 'But you're missing all this summer sunshine, especially down the shore. You should go for a dauner sometime. I was down there last night, early evening, and the sea at that time is so calm and relaxing. There's never any trouble around here, not that I've heard, but if you change your mind and want to go down, give me a call and I'll accompany you and Judith and Emmie. You'll be safe with me.'

The dressmaker smiled warmly and nodded. 'Yes, I'm sure we would, Calum. That's a very kind offer and I'll keep it in mind.'

Judith wondered if the dressmaker was just being polite because she hadn't ventured down to the sea in years. She certainly wasn't tied to the cottage, and the recent trips to the film premieres and television events in London were proof of that, but when the dressmaker was at home in the cottage, she never ventured far. She didn't even take part in the local summer fete, but she did contribute to the cost of the stalls.

'Where are you staying at the moment?' Judith asked him.

'At the postmaster's house. He's been kind enough to put me up. I'll be leaving fairly soon.' He glanced at Emmie. 'But I plan on coming back. It all depends on whether the fight works out, if you know what I mean.'

'If you win?' said Emmie.

'Or not,' he replied.

Judith glanced at the dressmaker wondering if she sensed the outcome of the boxing contest, but there was no hint either way from her expression.

Calum finished his ice cream and lemonade and sat back in his chair. 'Do I get a peek at these special dresses before I go?'

They'd all finished their tea, and the dressmaker nodded. 'Yes, let's have a look at them.'

Emmie went through to the sewing room, opened up one of the cases and lifted two of the dresses out. She'd hung them on padded clothes hangers after washing them and had kept the hangers in the shoulders when packing them. She carried them through and held them up. One dress was a classic rose print in various tones of pink and cream. It had a sweetheart neckline and was made from a soft cotton fabric. The other dress was a summery daisy and bee print. A beautiful button through design. Both of them were lovely and Emmie didn't know which one she preferred.

The dressmaker blinked, as if the memories attached to making the dresses were emotionally overwhelming. She'd expected to be reminded of her past, so long ago, when she'd first started out as a dress designer, but seeing them again, in such great condition, made her almost teary. But she fought against this, smiled and nodded. 'They look just the way I remember them.'

Calum stood up and went over for a closer look. 'I'm no expert when it comes to dresses, but these are beautiful.' He flicked a glance at Emmie as he said this, having a closer look at her too. The tea dress she was wearing emphasised her slender figure. She was so lovely and his heart ached just looking at her. He towered over her, as Hunter had done.

Emmie indicated the coded stitching on the inside of the necklines. 'These have the details I was telling you about,' she said to the dressmaker and handed one of them to her.

The dressmaker held it by the hanger and ran her hand down the fabric, remembering stitching the darts, fitting the short sleeves, finishing the hem.

'They've been well cared for,' Emmie explained, handing the other dress to Judith. 'Worn a few times I think, maybe for special occasions. I hand washed them.' She was used to washing vintage clothes and was careful when laundering them.

'Thank you for doing that, Emmie,' said the dressmaker. She sighed. 'I'm quite taken by how well they've kept their colour and styling.'

'I think they've been well–loved by whoever wore them,' Judith surmised. 'I'd know that they were your designs,' she said to the dressmaker. 'Even your first designs have your hallmark. The hand stitched finish on the hems, the cut and colours, the way you've used the classic floral fabrics to create something special.'

Emmie brought through two traditional tea dresses. One had a wrap over front and was made from a ditsy print fabric. The second was a gorgeous georgette blue and white polka dot dress with a sash that tied at the back of the waist.

The dressmaker reacted when she saw the polka dot dress. 'I loved this one, and almost kept it for myself.'

'No wonder you're making clothes for films and television shows,' said Calum, acknowledging her talent for dressmaking and design. He stepped forward and had a close–up look at the dresses.

The dressmaker smiled at him. 'I've been fortunate to work doing something I love all these years.' She held the polka dot dress and twirled it around on the hanger.

By now, Emmie had brought through a drop–waist dress with box pleats made from a soft, silky fabric with a lily of the valley print.

'I don't think you can get this fabric these days.' Judith sounded disheartened.

'It would definitely be on my wish list,' said Emmie. 'I love lily of the valley, and this fabric looks so classy.'

Calum sensed that the ladies wanted to talk about the dresses and knew it was time for him to leave. 'I'd better head out for my run. It was nice meeting you.' He included all three of them, hesitating when he smiled at Emmie. He was tempted to ask her out, maybe ask for her number so he could keep in contact with her. But he didn't want to embarrass her in front of the dressmaker and Judith. He'd ask her soon though. She was staying locally, so he'd see her again.

Emmie didn't pick up on the extent of Calum's admiration as she was so busy hanging up the dresses on a rail near the shelves of fabric. But the dressmaker certainly did.

The doorbell tinkled, startling Judith. 'We're not expecting any more deliveries,' she said, hurrying into the hallway.

The sound of Hunter's voice resonated through to the living room. 'I brought a copy of my new book for Emmie.'

Butterflies erupted inside Emmie. She felt excited that he'd come back, and the way he said her name made her heart flutter.

'Come away in, Hunter,' Judith said, welcoming him.

Hunter walked in carrying a book in his hand. He'd showered and now wore a clean white linen shirt, unbuttoned at the neck. He went over to Emmie. 'I wanted to give you this. I wasn't sure where you were staying and...' he shrugged, unsure what else to say.

The dressmaker cast a knowing look at Judith. Hunter's excuse was paper thin, unlike the book. A stylish spy thriller novel with his name embossed on the cover.

He flicked a glance at Calum, acknowledging that he was still there and hadn't gone for his run. Then he handed the book to Emmie.

She accepted it with thanks, taken aback that he'd brought it for her. The leading male character, a secret agent, was pictured standing in the shadows of a night scene cityscape. She was excited just looking at it. On the back cover was a brief summary of the story, and a picture of the author — Hunter, with a caption stating that this was the fourth book in his best selling international spy thriller series of novels.

Emmie gazed at the picture of Hunter, wearing a classic dark suit, his hair tamed but still sexy, his handsome face unsmiling, looking straight into the camera, causing her heart to jolt. The man standing here in the cottage wearing light summer clothes could morph into what looked like a secret agent himself. He wasn't of course, but the perception caught her off guard. Wow! Hunter looked amazing.

Calum sighed to himself, feeling his chances with Emmie fading as Hunter seemed to have captured her attention, and from the way he was looking at Emmie he was interested in her.

Judith sounded excited. 'I hope you've signed the book for her.'

Emmie blushed, thinking he wouldn't have given her a signed copy.

But Hunter nodded. 'I have.' His deep voice resonated in the living room.

Emmie opened the book and her heart fluttered when she read what he'd written on the title page. He'd signed it...but he'd written a message.

Judith made a bid to peek to see his signature, but Emmie sweetly closed the book and pretended she was overcome with excitement. Her blushes were real, but she hadn't anticipated a secret message from Hunter. She didn't want Judith to see it because she doubted Judith would hide her reaction. No, she wanted to keep this a secret for the moment.

Hunter looked at Emmie, seeking a reply, or a hint of her reaction.

Emmie rewound the words he'd written. 'To Emmie. Have dinner with me.' He'd signed his name and added his phone number.

His intense blue eyes were focussed on her, and all six foot plus of him stood there in front of her waiting on her response.

Emmie looked up at him and nodded as a blush burned across her cheeks.

This was all the reply he needed.

Judith fanned herself with a napkin. 'I don't know about you, but I think the day has become even hotter.'

Emmie's rosy cheeks confirmed that she agreed.

'Well, I'd better go for my run,' said Calum. 'I'm sure you ladies are eager to discuss your dresses.' He glanced at Hunter.

Hunter took the hint that he should leave too. 'I'll hopefully see you again soon.' His remark was made to all three women but particularly aimed at Emmie.

Judith accompanied Calum as he headed out. Hunter followed them.

At the front door Calum stepped outside, smiled at Judith and then got into his silver grey car, a stylish estate that had handled the rough forest terrain during the winter.

Hunter had left his bike at the cottage and driven up in his black sports car.

The two men acknowledged each other, though the jealous tension was clear to Judith. Behind her, Emmie hurried to the see them drive off.

'I think you've created a bit of rivalry between Hunter and Calum,' Judith said to her as she waved them off.

'I've no intention of getting involved with either of them, especially as I'm only here for a short break.'

'Your intentions may be fine, but when it comes to romance...' Judith shrugged.

Emmie watched the two cars drive off in different directions. Hunter drove back down to his cottage, while Calum headed further up into the forest. Then she followed Judith back into the living room where the dressmaker was studying the stitching on the dresses.

'I'll put the kettle on for tea.' Judith went into the kitchen and flicked the kettle on.

The dressmaker hung the polka dot dress on the rack and smiled knowingly at Emmie.

Emmie blushed. 'I don't know if I should have dinner with Hunter.'

This comment caused Judith to come hurrying through from the kitchen. 'What? Did I miss something?'

Emmie opened the book and showed Judith the message.

Judith giggled. 'That was a shrewd move by Hunter. No wonder you wouldn't let me see his signature.'

'I thought you'd say something in front of him, and Calum.'

'I would have.' She looked at the dressmaker. 'I was telling Emmie that she's caused a bit of rivalry between Hunter and Calum.'

'I'm not getting involved with either of them,' Emmie said unconvincingly.

They all laughed.

'What a pickle I could get myself into,' Emmie admitted.

'I think you already have, unless that smile and nod to Hunter meant nothing,' the dressmaker told her.

Emmie sighed. 'I may have inadvertently agreed to have dinner with him.'

The kettle started to boil. Judith hurried through to make the tea, but called out to Emmie. 'I want to hear all the details, and what you plan to do.'

'I've no idea what I'll do.' Emmie sat down and hoped the breeze wafting in from the patio would calm her senses. 'Hunter probably expects me to call him to arrange when we'll have dinner.' She shook her head in dismay. 'I'm not used be being so popular.'

'I'm sure you've had your fair share of romantic attention,' said the dressmaker.

'I suppose so, but...not from someone like Hunter, or Calum, both of them handsome and successful. Usually it's guys from work, or social acquaintances, and none of them have ever worked out happily. I've never been lucky when it comes to love.'

Judith made the tea quickly and hurried through with a freshly brewed pot and poured their tea.

'If you had to have dinner with one of them,' said Judith, 'would you prefer Hunter or Calum? Personally, I'd be in a dilemma over which one, though I'm not a lovely young woman like you, Emmie.'

'Calum is very likeable,' Emmie admitted.

The dressmaker sipped her tea. 'He is. I think he's an honest sort of young man. No guile, though perhaps life will eventually take the edge off his openness.'

'Do you think Hunter is a bit...wily?' Emmie asked.

'No, he's more experienced at keeping his emotions guarded,' said the dressmaker.

'Are you worried that he just wants you to wrinkle his duvet?' Judith asked.

Emmie almost choked on her tea.

'You know what I mean,' said Judith.

Emmie knew exactly what she meant. And this was concerning her.

'If Hunter can't be a gentleman on your first dinner date,' the dressmaker began, 'then he's not the man I think he is.'

'You think he's just hoping to have dinner?' Emmie asked her.

'I won't lie,' the dressmaker replied. 'But I don't think Hunter will try to sweet talk you into...wrinkling his duvet.'

They all laughed again, and the light–heartedness eased Emmie's concerns.

'I'm not naive,' said Emmie. 'I've had my share of bad dates and rotten relationships. But I really didn't expect this when I came here. I thought it would be a great few days away from the city. The chance to relax, walk along the shore, do a bit of embroidery and discuss the dresses with you.'

'You can still have all of that,' said the dressmaker. 'And perhaps make a couple of acquaintances that could lead to romance.'

'But I'm only here for a few days—'

The dressmaker cut–in. 'Maybe you'll be tempted to stay a little bit longer. The cottage down the shore is available.'

'What about my life in the city? I can't just give it up.'

'It would be silly to give it up on a whim or uncertainty,' the dressmaker told her. 'But could you put it on hold long enough to enjoy a break here? Enjoy the summer with us? I could certainly do with your help. I've a lot of pattern work and dressmaking to do.'

'I suppose I could phone my flatmate and tell her I'm going to stay for a longer holiday. She'll be happy to have the flat to herself and invite her boyfriend to stay while I'm away. And if I could continue making my embroidery patterns and selling them on my website, it wouldn't matter if I was living here or the city.'

'Something to think about,' Judith said to Emmie.

It was, and as the sun beat down outside the cottage, burnishing the garden in a hot summer glow, she wondered if she should enjoy a summer break by the sea. She had no one to answer to, and if she could sell her embroidery patterns while helping the dressmaker, it could work.

'You'll be paid well for helping me,' the dressmaker assured her.

'I wasn't thinking about that,' said Emmie.

'No, but I wanted you to take that into consideration.'

'I will.'

31

'Would you like to see some of the designs I'm working on?' the dressmaker asked Emmie.

'Yes, I'd love to.'

The dressmaker led the way through to the sewing room, followed by Emmie, Judith and Thimble.

The room was well–lit with light shining in the windows, but also from lamps that were set above the sewing tables. There were various sewing machines from the latest models to an old–fashioned treadle machine. On one table were paper pattern pieces sitting beside rolls of beautiful fabric.

Emmie's eyes widened when she saw the selection of silks, georgette, linen, cotton and velvet that were ready to be cut from the patterns. Then she noticed a large sketch book lying open on a table where the dressmaker had been sketching new designs.

'I love fashion drawings.' Emmie wished she had the talent to draw so well. She kept her hands off the sketch book, though she was tempted to flick through the contents to see the new designs.

'You're welcome to have a look,' the dressmaker offered. 'I'm not precious about my sketches. They're just pencil drawings and inked fashion illustrations.'

Emmie didn't need to be encouraged and eagerly began looking through the sketch book. Everything was beautifully drawn. 'These are so lovely they'd work well if framed as pieces of art.'

Judith was quick to agree. 'I've been telling her that for years. She should frame some of them and hang them up as artwork in the living room and the hallway.'

'Definitely, especially the black and white illustrations. They're so classy. I love fashion figures. And these are wonderful too.' Emmie indicated the dress designs that had been given a wash of watercolour to show the colour theme.

The dressmaker smiled and thanked Emmie for the compliments. 'Your embroidery designs, the floral patterns, are lovely too.'

Emmie accepted the compliment, but wasn't confident in her drawings. 'I'm okay at inking floral designs, but your fashion sketches...they're brilliant.'

Judith pulled down another large sketch book that was filled with the dressmaker's drawings of past designs. 'Look how many books are filled with the original dress pattern artwork.'

Emmie looked up at the shelf where a number of the books were stacked neatly. Years of work had been compiled into the books. She could happily spend an entire day looking through them, admiring the stylish illustrations and learning techniques to improve her own pattern making. But there was work to do. A lot of work. A television series was planned and the dressmaker had been hired to design and make the costumes, mainly dresses for the leading lady roles, and a few items for the leading men, including waistcoats.

'I'm not really into men's tailoring,' the dressmaker told Emmie. 'But these are part of the design package I've agreed to make for them.'

'When do they need to be ready?' Emmie asked.

'By the end of the summer, the beginning of the autumn. I've finished quite a few of the main costumes, the dresses for the leading ladies, but there are still a number of dresses to be cut and sewn.'

Emmie felt the excitement buzz inside her. She dearly wanted to be part of this, and yet...

'Stay a little while longer,' the dressmaker encouraged her.

Emmie needed no further encouragement as she gazed around the sewing room. It was the perfect room, filled with fine fabrics, artistic flair, a mini haberdashery that she could happily spend hours in mixing and matching buttons, ribbons and other trims, along with one of the most wonderful selection of threads she'd ever seen. She'd worked in a haberdashery and that shop was no match for what the dressmaker had tucked in boxes and shelves.

'I guess I'll be moving in here,' Emmie said lightly, though she would've happily done so. She'd always loved fabric and thread and... 'Is that a cupboard full of yarn?'

'That's my knitting stash,' said Judith. 'I often knit cardigans and wraps to go with the dresses.'

Emmie smiled. 'I'm sold. I'm staying. This is going to be an exciting summer.' Although sometimes she felt adrift, lost without any family or long–time friends to anchor her to anywhere, she bolstered herself thinking that there was a benefit to being on her own. She was her own boss, with no ties, and could do what she wanted. The trip to the dressmaker's cottage had started out as a small holiday, but she could extend her plans to stay until the dressmaking was done. A summer working on her embroidery patterns and stitching dresses while living in a cottage by the sea sounded wonderful.

And then she thought about Hunter. If she was here for the summer, would she be prepared to date him?

As the dressmaker showed her what needed to be done, and they started working together, she didn't have time to think about what she'd do when it came to Hunter. Or Calum for that matter. The way he'd looked at her with those green eyes...

'Emmie, could you unroll this satin and prepare to cut out the pattern pieces?' the dressmaker's voice interrupted her thoughts, and continued to do so as they worked all afternoon on the designs.

CHAPTER FOUR

Sewing Bee Night

Calum ran through the forest, burning off his excess energy and tension — but no matter how he tried, he couldn't shake off thinking about Emmie. He hadn't dated any woman in a while. His busy training schedule and unsettled lifestyle didn't allow much time for romance. He'd always wanted a relationship like his parents had, but he'd never met anyone that he felt he'd like to settle down with. And although he'd only just met Emmie, he'd been attracted to her the moment he saw her. He shrugged off the feeling and kept on running.

He'd parked his car in a part of the forest he was familiar with. He'd used this route during the winter. Now it looked lush with greenery. The scent was exhilarating, and with it being higher up, right in the heart of the forest, the air was the coolest he was going to get on a hot day like this.

He glimpsed bramble cottage through the trees, but didn't venture near it. The people living in it could mistake him for some sort of intruder, or a man up to no good. He wished he could've stayed there again. Maybe some other time, preferably when Emmie was here again too.

He shook the thoughts away and put on a spurt of speed, running through the forest, burning up all that pent up energy...

Hunter felt so hot when he got back to the cottage that he took his shirt off and wandered around barefoot with only his jeans on. He padded around, feeling like a caged tiger with so much on his mind and an unsettled sense that he'd overstepped the mark with Emmie. The book had been the only thing he could think of as an excuse to go back to the dressmaker's cottage. But was his bold invitation a step too far? And was Emmie attracted to Calum?

He ran a frustrated hand through his hair, pushing it back from his troubled brow, wishing he'd handled things better, hoping that Calum wouldn't be on the scene for long. He was encouraged by the idea that Emmie seemed happy ensconced in the dressmaker's cottage and maybe she'd stay longer than she'd originally intended. And he wished she would call him. Or text him, and put him out of his misery wondering if the secret nod she'd given him wasn't her acceptance to have dinner with him after all. Had he read too much into her response?

He poured a long, cold glass of water, added some ice, and then sat outside in the garden under the shade of one of the trees. The grass felt cool on his bare feet and the scent of the flowers and greenery soothed his senses.

As he sat there, ideas for his new book, the one he was working on, started to filter through, and he went inside, opened his laptop, and began to hammer notes, snippets of dialogue, into the latest chapter. He'd been stuck on this chapter, unsure how to convey the sense of covert excitement that was needed for the type of spy thriller novel he was writing.

He wrote until he couldn't keep up with the thoughts and ideas racing through his mind.

Finally, he closed the laptop, realising the day was done, and had been replaced by a glorious early evening glow. The air was still warm, but the intense heat had eased off.

He looked at the time. Dinner time in his world. He checked his phone for text messages, missed calls and—

He stopped and shook the urgency from his tense muscles. Emmie hadn't contacted him. Maybe he'd misread her reaction to his dinner invitation. For a moment, his heart felt heavy, but then he wondered if she was still busy sewing and planned to call him later to arrange dinner for another night.

Feeling hopeful, he threw his shirt on, jumped in his car and drove down to the shore to check out the small restaurant he'd seen but never frequented. Since he'd arrived, he'd bought groceries from the local shop and cooked for himself, nothing fancy, especially in this weather — salad weather, with a modicum of salmon, chicken and pasta.

He parked down by the shore and walked along the esplanade enjoying the warm sea air. The sea sparkled, enticing him to go for a swim, but he decided to view the restaurant's menu that was posted outside the front window. The menu was impressive and he thought this would be perfect for dinner with Emmie. Or perhaps he could drive her to the city for a night out at one of his favourite restaurants and then take in a show. He took a deep breath and stopped himself planning for things that may not happen, and probably the last thing Emmie wanted was to have a night out in the city when she'd come here to get away from the hustle and bustle.

As he walked back to his car a woman called out to him from the bookshop. 'Excuse me, Hunter.' Bea, the bookshop owner smiled hopefully at him. Bea had inquisitive green eyes and silky, shoulder length titian hair. She was in her early thirties with pretty, pale features. 'I wondered if you could sign a few copies of your new book. Customers like to buy a signed copy.' Bea had met him before in the bookshop and he'd signed a handful of books, but these had been snapped up. 'I ordered more copies, and I was hoping to snare you if I saw you.' She smiled, joking with him.

'Yes, I'd be happy to,' he confirmed, and headed into the bookshop with Bea.

He just missed seeing Emmie drive up to the strawberry jam cottage nearby. A pretty cottage that looked pale pink in the early evening glow. She'd followed Judith in her car leading the way down to the shore.

Emmie smiled when she saw the cottage. 'It looks lovely.'

'Wait until you see inside.' Judith opened the unlocked front door and showed Emmie around the two bedroom property.

'Oh, it's perfect.' Emmie admired the decor, a mix of traditional and modern. The living room had a fireplace, was bright and airy, but she pictured it would be cosy in the winter. Quilts adorned the sofa and chairs, and the atmosphere was homely.

Judith led her through to the kitchen. 'The cupboards and the fridge are stocked with groceries. There's fresh milk, butter, cheese, bread and scones. And there's a grocery shop near the post office.'

Emmie loved the kitchen. Pretty strawberry print curtains were tied up with ribbons on the window. Floral print accessories such as the cushions on the chairs and oven mitt created a modern vintage look, and she noted a hint of strawberry jam scent in the air. She peered out the window at the garden. 'A garden too.' There were cherry trees, a small lawn and lots of summer flowers.

'It's a proper wee home from home. All the bedding and linen is fresh and clean and there's a sewing machine set up in the living room if you need it.'

'I love it.'

Judith checked the time. 'Remember, the sewing bee is on tonight. Ethel's cottage is the pale blue one just along the esplanade, and I live further along from that. I sent a message to tell her you'll be there.'

'I'm looking forward to the sewing bee.'

'The ladies will be delighted to meet you.' She hesitated. 'Maybe you should phone Hunter, let him know you're busy this evening. I'm sure he's wondering if you'll have dinner with him.'

Emmie nodded, checked the number he'd written in the book, and phoned him.

Hunter was still in the bookshop signing copies of his novel when she called.

'Hunter?' She wondered if he heard the nervousness in her voice.

'Emmie. I'm eh...in the bookshop at the moment.'

Realising the call wouldn't be private, she kept her voice down and told him her plans. 'I'd like to have dinner, but I'm going to the sewing bee tonight.'

'How about tomorrow night?'

'Yes, that would be fine.'

'I'll pick you up at seven.'

'See you then.' She finished the call and smiled at Judith.

'It sounds like you've got a dinner date.'

Emmie nodded. 'Tomorrow night.'

'There's a local summer barbeque event down on the shore tomorrow night. Maybe you could enjoy yourselves there,' Judith suggested. 'Unless Hunter's planning on wining and dining you in a restaurant.'

'A barbeque with lots of local people there would be ideal. Less intimate. Until I get to know him better and whether or not I want to get involved.' Emmie looked at her phone, deciding whether to call him.

Judith nodded her encouragement. 'Tell him now before he makes a restaurant booking.'

Emmie called him. 'Hi, me again. Judith's just told me there's a summer barbecue down the shore tomorrow night.'

'Want to go?' he asked before she could suggest it.

'Yes, it sounds like fun. And it may be a better...' she hesitated.

'First date?'

Emmie blushed even though he couldn't see her. Her heart pounded so loud she wondered if he could hear it. He probably sensed her reaction.

'I'll still pick you up at seven. Where exactly are you staying?'

'At the strawberry jam cottage. The pale pink cottage near the shops and post office.'

'I know the one. I'll be there at seven.'

After the call, Emmie's cheeks were still burning. 'I hope I'm doing the right thing. I really had no intention of dating anyone. This could go so wrong.'

'You have to take a chance on finding happiness. I was happily married for more than twenty–five years, and since he passed a few years ago, I still miss him. But I have a great life here. So I'd advise you to keep your heart open to romance.'

Emmie nodded. 'Thanks, Judith. I will.'

Judith took a deep breath. 'Right, I'd better go and let you settle in. I'll see you at the sewing bee. Remember to bring your embroidery. I don't know if you'll get much embroidery done because it's going to be a lively evening.'

'As in fun?' Emmie pictured a chatty night with the ladies, but relaxing with their sewing and knitting.

'There will be plenty of fun. Aurora runs a magazine, an online publication, that's filled with craft features. Everything from quilting to dressmaking, knitting to pressed flowers, crochet to scrapbooking.'

'A magazine?'

'Yes. Aurora was brought up here, but then went to work in London for years in the magazine world, so she knows the business well. She came back to start up her own online craft magazine, and asked us to help provide patterns, recipes, and take part in the features. It's very popular. We all benefit from contributing our patterns for the features. Aurora credits us and includes links to our websites, so we've all been busier. Ethel sells a lot more of her hand dyed yarn since she's been involved in the monthly features. I've given Aurora knitting patterns and had orders to knit items. I'm not even in business like Ethel, or Hilda, a quilter, or some of the other ladies that sell their sewing and crafts. Even Bea's bookshop feature was a success, especially as she makes pressed flower books as well as selling novels, like Hunter's books.'

'It sounds like a great magazine.'

'It is. People are enjoying the patterns, quilting and sewing tips, special offers, and all the advertising is done in features. Aurora will no doubt want embroidery patterns from you when she finds out that you design patterns. So if she offers you a feature say yes. Trust me. You'll do well from it.'

Emmie nodded as Judith continued to tell her about Aurora.

'She's now married to Bredon the beemaster. They live in his cottage.' Judith paused. 'Aurora is a magnet for trouble. Always has been. But she wants the best for all of us, and we need someone like her to pull the magazine together every month.'

'Do you think maybe I'll be in the way tonight at the sewing bee if you're all so busy? I don't mind. I could pop along next time,' she offered.

'No, it's perfect. You'll meet everybody and it'll let you see what we're all up to.'

Emmie nodded. 'Okay, great.'

'Right, I'm away this time. See you later. Remember, Ethel's cottage is the pale blue one with a lovely wee garden full of flowers. It's one of the oldest cottages in the area.'

And off she went, waving happily and driving away along the esplanade.

As she waved to Judith, Emmie noticed the sleek, black sports car parked nearby. Then she saw Hunter coming out of the bookshop and striding over to his car.

'It's a fine night, Emmie,' a man's voice said, startling her.

She glanced round and saw Calum walking towards her. He was carrying a large bag of groceries.

'I'm cooking something tasty for the postmaster's dinner. He won't take payment for letting me stay in his house, so I treat him to a delicious dinner every night.'

'If you're as good a chef as I think you are, I bet the postmaster prefers to be paid in tasty dinners.'

'I didn't mean to sound over confident when I mentioned my cooking earlier.'

'You didn't,' she assured him. 'I get the impression that whatever you do, whether it's cooking or training or boxing, you give it all you've got.'

'I try to.'

There was a pause as he went to saying something, and then noticed her glance over at Hunter getting into his car.

'Hunter has invited me to go to the summer barbecue,' she said, feeling she needed to tell him. She sensed he was attracted to her, and she admitted that he was handsome.

'I'll probably see you there. I'm helping with the cooking.'

'Oh, well I'll definitely see you.'

There was another pause, and again she sensed a frisson of excitement between them.

'I'd better get the dinner cooked for the postmaster.' He smiled and walked away. Then he paused and called to her. 'Maybe one night, if you've got time, I could cook dinner for you.'

Emmie found herself nodding without any real commitment, and then watched the tall, broad shouldered figure of Calum walk away. She glanced at Hunter's dark car driving off. Hunter hadn't noticed her, or if he had, he didn't wave or acknowledge that he'd seen her. Butterflies of excitement charged through her at the thought of her date with him, and she was looking forward to the sewing bee.

Glancing again at the black car disappearing into the distance, she went inside the cottage and got ready for the sewing bee night.

Hunter wrung out his frustration on the driving wheel as he drove away from the shore and up to his cottage.

He rewound the scene — Emmie standing there, smiling at Calum. They looked happy together. He wondered what Calum was telling her.

The more he thought about Emmie when he was back at his cottage and trying to continue with his writing, he realised something — Emmie reminded him of someone. The heroine in the first book of his spy series was like Emmie. He'd described his perfect women, in character, attitude and looks. Maybe that was why he felt so attracted to her. There was something about her...he sensed it was perhaps her uncanny likeness to his leading lady. At the end of the first novel, her character didn't end up with the lead guy. He'd kept their romance unfinished, and she hadn't been included in the next three books in the series. But maybe he could bring her back into the story. Perhaps she was the missing element he needed to balance the romance and excitement and adventure in his latest book.

41

He planned to tell Emmie about this when he picked her up to go to the barbecue. Hopefully she'd take it as a compliment that she was similar to the heroine in the series. A creative, artistic, hardworking young woman, naturally beautiful. Through circumstances, she becomes involved in the secretive world of the spying game, something she wasn't ever part of before. He'd created a character that was his ideal woman. Now he'd met someone like her for real. But the figure of Calum loomed in his thoughts. He sensed that Calum would make a play for Emmie, and he'd have to make sure that he didn't let her slip through his fingers into Calum's life. He didn't know what he'd have to do to achieve this, but starting out with a date to the barbecue felt exciting.

He settled down to write as ideas flooded his thoughts, and included the first scene with the original heroine. The element of romance in his action–packed spy novels was what helped make his books popular.

He pictured the heroine. A young woman, like Emmie, strong but vulnerable, naturally beautiful with a sexy little figure he wanted to claim with every sinew of his masculine body.

Scolding himself for letting his imagination run wild, he continued writing as the evening light faded into the night.

Emmie tucked her embroidery into her bag, a craft bag she'd made herself that had a sewing theme motif embroidered on it. She'd freshened her make up, brushed her hair and felt too excited to cook a full dinner so she'd opted for a cup of tea and a toasted cheese scone with a crisp green salad and cherry tomatoes.

She put Hunter's book in the living room beside the sewing machine, along with the large sketch book filled with the dressmaker's fashion illustrations — the original artwork. The dressmaker had entrusted her with it after they'd finished the pattern cutting and sewing, suggesting she familiarised herself with the styling that would be used for the dresses they had to design for the television series.

Although she wanted to go to the sewing bee, she was tempted to stay and study the dressmaker's sketch book. It was filled with notes on stitching and details about the patterns. And this was just one of the books that the dressmaker had. There were so many things to learn and read about. Sighing, she put the sketch book down, picked up her bag and headed out.

The sea shimmered as she walked the short distance along the esplanade to Ethel's cottage. A warm sea breeze wafted in from the distant islands to the shore. The fresh, salty scent of the sea was in stark contrast to the heady floral fragrance of the forest. She stopped to gaze around her at the seashore scenery. She was a fraction early, so there was time to pause and take in her surroundings.

Two boats were highlighted against the shimmering sea — one was an expensive looking boat sailing into the little harbour and the other, a large white yacht with blue and white sails, headed along the coast.

Bea stood outside her bookshop waving, welcoming the man sailing into the harbour. Lewis, a fine looking man, waved back to Bea.

Emmie didn't know either of them, but she imagined they were a loving young couple.

Meanwhile, Fintry the flower hunter sailed his yacht along the coast, enjoying the twilight summer with his fiancée Mairead.

The shops had closed for the day, but lights glowed from the bar restaurant. The area was a hub of calm and cosy community as the evening deepened.

A handful of people were making the most of the hot summer night and were frolicking and having fun down on the sand. A tall, strapping man stripped to the waist and wearing a kilt picked up a pretty and petite young blonde woman and twirled her around his head before playfully threatening to throw her into the sea. Her giggling and joyous laughter made Emmie smile. They looked like a happy couple.

A pang of longing to have such a relationship jarred her, and she walked on along the esplanade. The couples she'd seen were all around the same age as her, and she wondered if she'd ever feel settled. Pushing her doubts aside, she headed towards Ethel's cottage.

The front door was open, and lights glowed from inside, making it look welcoming.

Two women were heading inside, armed with craft bags filled with their latest sewing and knitting projects. Their cheerful chatter wafted through the calm night air. Emmie followed them inside.

The living room was abuzz with ladies busy settling down for the evening's sewing bee. It was comfy and cosy, but it was clearly a yarn lover's house, a working house where the living room had an extension out to the spacious back garden. The room was brimming with skeins of hand dyed yarn on a display rack at one end. Shelves were stacked with colourful yarn ranging from aqua blues and to the palest sea foam, cerise to cherry, amethyst to heather. The neutral colours were equally enticing with stormy sky grey to silvery shades and beautiful beige tones. Two spinning wheels sat beside the fireplace, and knitting patterns and samples of Ethel's new yarns were displayed on a table.

The clatter of tea cups and teaspoons sounded from the kitchen, accompanied by chatter and laughter.

Emmie paused for a moment to take it all in, glad she'd been invited.

Ethel spotted the newcomer and smiled at her. 'You must be Emmie. Judith told me you'd be here. She hasn't arrived yet, but she'll be here soon.'

Ethel was in her retirement years and wore her silvery blonde hair pinned up in a tidy bun. Despite the heat, she wore a lace weight shawl around her shoulders, knitted in shades of blue from one of the latest ranges of her yarn.

Emmie gazed around at the colourful array of yarn on the shelves, and the spinning wheels. 'Judith says you spin and dye your own yarn.'

'Yes, and although this is the sewing bee, we do all sorts of crafts including knitting and crochet. But tonight we're helping Aurora with the magazine features.'

'Judith told me about Aurora and the magazine.'

'She's taking pictures of one of the models for the knitwear feature.' Ethel sounded excited. 'I knitted a cardigan and a jumper. The patterns are going to be in the magazine.'

Ethel then introduced Emmie to everyone. 'This is Emmie. She's joining the bee. She's working with the dressmaker, and staying at the strawberry jam cottage.'

Numerous members smiled and bid her welcome, and introductions were made.

Hilda hurried over with a tray of tea. 'Would you like a cup of tea, Emmie?' Hilda was helping organise the tea along with a couple

44

of other ladies. Similar in age to Ethel, her brown hair had glitter strands, and she was fit and strong. Her cotton dress was one she'd made years ago and brought out during hot summer days to wear with sensible shoes.

'Yes, thank you.' Emmie barely had time to take a sip when Judith arrived with Ione and Bea.

'This is Bea. She owns the bookshop,' said Judith, taking over the introductions while Ethel scurried around organising things for the photo–shoot.

Emmie smiled at Bea. 'Pleased to meet you.' She didn't mention that she'd seen her outside the bookshop.

'I'm quite a new member too,' Bea told her.

'And this is Ione,' Judith added. 'Ione recently married Big Sam our local silversmith.'

'The man wearing the kilt down the shore?' said Emmie. 'I saw him twirling you above his head.'

Ione giggled and her wide blue eyes shone with delight. 'He's full of fun.'

'Are you a quilter?' Bea asked Emmie, noting the fabric peeping out from her bag.

'No, an embroiderer, and I like dressmaking, especially upcycling vintage dresses and pre–loved fashion.'

They'd just started talking about make do and mend, and how Ione used scraps of fabric to make her patchwork fairy dolls, when Aurora arrived. Her shiny chestnut hair, blunt cut and straight, tipped her shoulders. In her thirties, she wore a navy and white polka dot dress and pumps, and had retained the sophisticated and well–groomed look she'd worn for years during her media work in London. Her alert blue eyes skimmed the faces in the room noting it was busy.

'Sorry I'm late, again,' Aurora apologised, bursting in, brimming with energy and a sense of being mildly harassed. 'It's close to the deadline for this month's issue of the magazine. So my world is full of crafty chaos at the moment.'

Aurora started to unpack one of the three bags she was loaded with. She showed the ladies some printouts of the features that were to be put into the magazine. 'This is your latest pressed flower books article,' she said to Bea. 'And Hilda's patchwork quilt pattern is one of the highlights on the front cover.'

45

'My quilt's going on the front cover of the magazine?' Hilda sounded thrilled.

Aurora nodded. 'The bright, fresh colours are ideal.'

Ethel smiled at Hilda, pleased for her friend's chance to be on the cover.

'We've got a new member,' Ethel told Aurora. 'Emmie is joining us for the summer.'

Aurora's smile was warm and genuine. 'What crafts are you into?'

Emmie glanced at Judith, and then said, 'I design embroidery patterns.'

Aurora's face lit up with glee. 'Perfect. We need a new embroidery feature. Do you have any patterns you'd like to contribute? Have the ladies told you about the magazine?'

'Judith told me about it, and I'd be happy to give you embroidery patterns for your magazine.'

'Brilliant.'

Emmie showed her the embroidery she'd been working on. 'These are some of my floral designs.'

'These are so pretty. Could you email the patterns and any pics you have of the embroideries?'

Emmie nodded and they exchanged details and agreed what was needed.

'I'll email you a copy of our pagination for this issue,' said Aurora. 'It'll let you see what the content is for this month.'

'I've put two spinning wheels beside the fireside,' Ethel said to Aurora. 'The others are over near the yarn display, and you can move them to suit whatever you want for the photos.' There was an urgency in her tone.

Aurora checked the time. 'Our model should be here soon. Do you have the knitwear ready? I'd like to start with pics of the cardigan then the jumper.'

'I do,' said Ethel, and then hurried over to adjust one of the spinning wheels so that the yarn would show in the photographs.

As the whirlwind circled around Emmie, she sipped her tea and got caught up in the sense of excitement, especially as her embroidery patterns were now going to be featured in the magazine. She felt part of the sewing bee and she hadn't even sewn anything.

Emmie glanced over at two members sitting at their sewing machines, stitching like lightning. Both of them were working on what appeared to be items of clothing made from beautiful deep blue satin. Emmie wasn't sure what they were making, possibly a gorgeous silky satin dressing gown and a belt to go with it. She wondered if the model was going to wear it, and this was contributing to the sense of urgency to get it finished in time for the photo–shoot.

'They're expert seamstresses,' said Ethel, seeing the inquisitive expression on Emmie's face. 'The hem on the gown was too long. They're making a last minute alteration. And they needed toggles on the belt to go with it.'

The whirring stopped at the same time as a knock sounded from the front door of the cottage.

The model had arrived.

CHAPTER FIVE

Model Material

Calum stood at the front door of Ethel's cottage, accompanied by the postmaster.

'I can't believe I let you talk me into this.' Calum sounded anxious.

'The sewing bee ladies have been kind enough to make you a new robe for your boxing match. You'll make quite an entrance in the ring wearing it. Ethel gave me a sneak peek and it reminds me of the classic boxing robes fighters wore at the championship shows I used to go to when I was a young scrapper.'

'I appreciate the ladies making it. I really do, but...' Calum bounced anxiously on the spot, as if about to step into the fray. 'I didn't think they'd want me to model knitwear for their magazine. I'm not model material.'

'It'll mean the world to them to have a champion like yourself featured in their magazine. Aurora is an expert from her years of magazine work in London. She'll make sure the feature is a corker.'

Calum didn't doubt that it would look great, but he'd heard tales that the sewing bee ladies could be quite mischievous.

'And it keeps me in the good books with Ethel,' said the postmaster. 'When Ethel asked me to help them find a man to model their men's knitwear, I thought you'd be ideal. A fit, young man like yourself. It was Aurora's idea to expand on the knitting pattern feature and include an interview with you for the magazine. The boxing robe is a thank you for doing it. Remember, I'm here as your backup.'

Calum nodded and continued to step edgily as if ready to make a run for it.

The postmaster smiled and nudged him. 'Last chance to run.'

'Run?' Aurora's wide blue eyes looked at them as she opened the door.

Ethel frowned at the postmaster.

'I was talking to Calum about his training. He's thinking of going for a run later,' the postmaster waffled to the ladies. Aurora believed him, but Ethel was wise to his ploys. However, she said nothing as Calum was welcomed inside.

Aurora swept Calum through to the living room where the ladies smiled and were excited to see him.

'I thought you might have chickened out,' Aurora said to Calum.

'He's a boxer, Aurora,' the postmaster reminded her. 'He doesn't sprout chicken feathers even when faced with a room full of sewing bee ladies.'

Calum laughed nervously. And that's when he saw Emmie looking at him, taken aback that he was the knitwear model. He wasn't sure if this made him feel less or more nervous to see her there. He nodded and smiled. 'Emmie.'

She smiled back at him.

The women glanced at Emmie, surprised that she was acquainted with him, as she was the newcomer. For some of them, this was their first glimpse of the strapping boxer, but he'd been well talked about.

'You know Calum?' Ione whispered over Emmie's shoulder.

Before Emmie could explain, someone else cut–in on the conversation.

'Emmie met him this afternoon at the dressmaker's cottage,' said Judith.

'This is the first time I've had a proper look at him,' Ione told them. 'He's quite elusive, always running through the forest.' She appraised him and nodded. 'He's very fit and handsome, isn't he? Someone will snap him up if he lives here any longer. Not me of course.' She touched her wedding ring, still feeling the excitement of being a new bride. Big Sam's wife.

'He's very nice,' Emmie agreed.

Ione smiled. 'Maybe it'll be you, Emmie. I saw the way Calum looked at you.'

'We think he's got a wee fancy for Emmie,' Judith whispered.

'Judith!' Emmie scolded her quietly.

Judith brushed the scolding aside. 'Well, he does.'

Ione frowned at Emmie. 'There's many a woman would jump at the chance of dating Calum.'

'But Emmie's got a dinner date with Hunter,' Judith confided to Ione.

Emmie started to blush. 'I'm only going with him to the barbecue.'

'You're dating Hunter!' Ione's astounded tone pierced through the chatter causing the ladies to stare at Emmie. But Emmie only noticed the reaction on Calum's face. Disappointment. He'd missed his chance.

Aurora rubbed her hands together gleefully. 'Okay, Calum, let's get your clothes off and take these pictures.'

She could've chosen her words better so as not to cause Calum's heart rate to skyrocket, but she quickly explained.

'What I mean is, get you into the knitwear. We're starting with the men's chunky knit cardigan. It has a shawl collar. We'd like to emphasise that it's versatile and can be worn on its own without a top showing underneath at the neckline.'

'You want me to just wear the cardigan on its own?' Calum clarified.

'If you don't mind.' Aurora pointed through to another room. 'You can change in there while we set up the lighting.'

Calum looked like he couldn't wait to step out of the focus of attention and hurried through to the room.

'I've hung the knitwear on a rail,' Ethel called through to him. 'They're hanging in the right order. Three items. The first one is the wild sea grey cardigan.' Ethel then explained quickly to Emmie. 'The seashore and stormy grey yarns are part of my new collections.' She reached over to a shelf and handed Emmie a sample card with all the new tones of grey yarn.

'These are so classy,' said Emmie, wishing she could knit something with at least two of the gorgeous grey tones even though she wasn't really a great knitter.

Aurora set up her camera while joining in the conversation. 'The texture and variegated shades of grey evoke a sense of atmosphere — the stormy skies that rage over the sea, along the coast and out to the islands.' Aurora sounded as if she was in feature writing mode, but Emmie got the feeling of it. The yarn was enticing.

'I've got a wee sample pack tucked away for you, Emmie,' said Ethel. 'I'll give it to you later.'

'Thank you, Ethel.' Emmie wondered if she would attempt to knit something, anything, just to feel the beautiful texture and colour of the new hand dyed yarn that Ethel had spun expertly herself. She could see why Ethel's yarn was so popular.

Calum stepped out into the living room, adjusting the cardigan, slightly nervous, but he'd given himself a pep talk while getting changed, like he did before a fight. Stay strong, be calm, focus on what you need to do, what you're capable of. It worked. He felt less anxious. But the sewing bee members reaction when they saw him set his nerves jangling again.

Cheers and applause erupted as the ladies admired the tall, handsome figure standing there in his dark, grey jeans that emphasised his fit build. The cardigan's styling looked great on him. The shawl collar gave them a peek at his smooth chest and highlighted his broad shoulders.

'Where do you want me to stand?' Calum pushed the sleeves up casually, and with his dark hair slightly ruffled and strands falling over his brow, emphasising his green eyes, he made a classic piece of knitwear look sexy.

One of the ladies jokingly fanned herself with a knitting pattern, and there were giggles and cheers throughout the members.

The postmaster pressed himself well out of the way near the back window and cheekily stole a piece of shortbread from their cake stand.

'Over at the fireplace, beside one of the spinning wheels,' Aurora told him, flicking on a lamp to help create a cosy atmosphere. 'We want to show that the yarn is hand spun by Ethel.'

Calum understood and leaned on the old–fashioned mantlepiece, while propping one booted foot on the tiles in front of the fire. The fire wasn't lit. It was too hot an evening, but it was stacked ready with logs and worked well to set the scene.

His manly stature looked great and created just the look Aurora had in mind. 'You're a natural, Calum,' she complimented him.

He smiled and she captured the genuine warmth and twinkle in those beautiful green eyes of his.

Aurora checked the images on her camera, showing them to Ethel. 'These look amazing.'

'My fireplace looks a treat in the pictures, and Calum seems right at home.' Ethel sounded delighted.

Several women snatched a peek at the pictures, including Emmie.

Calum stepped close and gazed over her shoulder at the images.

51

His closeness set Emmie's heart racing, especially when she glanced round and up at him. So tall and handsome, she thought with such a cute, sexy smile.

Calum's nerves were calmer now, and he settled quickly into the hustle and bustle of the sewing bee ladies as they buzzed around him, asking about his training, and whether he thought he'd win his next fight.

'The training is going well,' he said. 'I'll do my utmost in the next fight.'

'We're backing you all the way,' one of the ladies called over to him.

He smiled his thanks, but kept glancing at Emmie. Her approval was what mattered most to him.

'What's it like to run through the forest?' Ione asked him, smiling excitedly at the thought of it. 'It sounds wild and wonderful. I hardly ever go up to the forest, and never on my own. I'd definitely get lost.'

'I love the forest,' Calum told her. 'I lived in Bramble cottage during the winter for a short time when I was training for a previous contest, so I sort of know my way around it.'

'I've seen films where boxers run along the shore to do their training,' said Hilda. 'My sister, Jessie, is very fit and strong. She does cartwheels on the sand, just for fun. But I think she'd draw the line at running through the forest, especially in the winter, when it's darker.'

'The forest was covered in snow the last time I was here,' he explained. 'I loved running through it with all the trees white with snow.'

Aurora and Ethel were setting up the spinning wheels in another part of the living room beside the main yarn display rack and shelves stacked with colourful yarn.

'The jumper is next,' Aurora told Calum.

'I'll change into it,' he said, and went through to put it on.

Aurora viewed the scene through the lens. 'The display rack will create a wall of vibrant colour as the background. It'll make for a wonderful shot.'

Calum emerged wearing a classic, round neck jumper with cable knit details. This was in storm grey to light silvery grey. Ethel had designed the pattern and knitted the jumper, and the cardigan.

'This is a great design, Ethel.' By now, Calum was on first name terms with the ladies.

And the postmaster was on to his first cup of tea and second piece of shortbread.

Ethel beamed, delighted at the compliment.

'Could you stand over at the yarn display please,' said Aurora.

The display rack was almost as tall as Calum. He stood in front of it, strong and steady, looking right into the camera.

Aurora clicked the camera into action, capturing his intense gaze before he started to smile. His good natured personality kept shining through along with his natural inclination to smile rather than look moody. But sometimes, especially when he glanced at Emmie, the intensity burned through, the longing to rewind time and have asked Emmie for a date before Hunter beat him to it. The fighter in him viewed it like moves — engage with his opponent, strike first, go for the win, no hesitation. *No hesitation.* This had always been one of his fighting tactics that had taken him to a championship level. But he'd hesitated when it came to Emmie. If he'd been bolder, would it be him she was going to the barbecue with? Or was her interest in Hunter already too strong?

'You're looking wonderful,' Aurora told him. She didn't say, but the depths of his expressions showed in his eyes. Such soulful and beautiful eyes for a man. What was running through his thoughts she wondered? Whatever it was gave glimpses of hope mixed with triumph and then defeat. She'd never seen any man look like that in the photos she'd taken of them. And she'd done this for years.

'These are brilliant,' Aurora finally announced, flicking through the images on her camera. 'This feature will look incredible.' She handed him a couple of pages she'd printed out from the forthcoming magazine feature. 'I've written the editorial. Have a read through it. Once you've approved it, that's what will go in the magazine along with the pics.'

Calum skimmed what she'd written. 'This is very flattering,' he said with a smile.

'I checked the information about your background, training and contests from your website, so these should be accurate. The rest is why you're here, honing your training, in our wee community, getting ready for your fight. And we're running a competition in the magazine to win the cardigan you were wearing,' said Aurora. 'If that's okay with you?'

'Yes, fine,' he agreed.

Aurora smiled at him. 'We're keeping the jumper to raffle it at our next fete.'

Calum nodded again. 'Sounds ideal.'

'Have a sit down and a cuppa while you read the feature properly,' Ethel suggested, ushering him over to a seat.

Calum sat down, stretching his long legs out, still wearing the jumper, and read the two pages of editorial, smiling and nodding his approval.

Hilda brought him a cup of tea while Ethel gave him one of her fresh baked scones. She sat it down on the table next to him.

Calum took a sip of tea as he read the last paragraph, and then bit into the scone. He'd been so nervous about going to the sewing bee that he'd hardly eaten any of the lemon baked salmon dinner he'd cooked for the postmaster.

'I love the taste and texture of this scone,' said Calum. 'What's your secret ingredient, Ethel?'

'Buttermilk,' Ethel revealed.

'Do you have the recipe?' Calum asked her.

Ethel blinked. 'Eh, yes. I'll give you a copy of it.'

'Great.'

'Are you into baking?' Ethel asked him.

'Baking, cooking...I trained as a chef and plan to have my own restaurant once the boxing's done.'

The women were interested. A handsome man who could fight and cook. Oh yes, they liked Calum.

'I didn't know that.' Ethel gave the postmaster the eye, as if he should've told her, but he looked as surprised as the others.

'Not many people realise my future plans involve cooking.'

'I'll give you the scone recipe,' Ethel told Calum.

'And your shortbread recipe,' the postmaster requested. 'If Calum wants to practise making shortbread, I'd be happy to be his tester,' the postmaster added with laughter in his tone.

'I think he's hinting,' Calum said to Ethel.

'Subtle as a sledgehammer as always.' Ethel went through to the kitchen where she kept her recipes. She scanned and printed them out for him on her printer as if it they were her knitting patterns,

54

while Aurora downloaded the photos on to her laptop and everyone gathered round to have a look.

Ethel gave the recipes to the postmaster for safe keeping, as Calum went through to get changed into the long sleeve, knitted hoody.

'This next item isn't part of the magazine feature,' Ethel confided to Emmie.

'What's it for?' asked Emmie.

'I asked Ethel to knit it for Calum,' said the postmaster. 'I want to give him a wee gift before he leaves. I used to have one when I was into the boxing training and it was so handy. I wish I still had it, or maybe someone would knit me a new one.' He grinned at Ethel.

'He's so subtle, isn't he?' Ethel said to Emmie.

They all laughed.

Calum put the hoody on. It was a perfect fit, and so comfortable. As if it was made for him. The yarn was soft and yet he felt it would be perfect for running and training in all weathers. He liked the cardigan and the jumper, but the hoody...he loved it. And it was knitted in his favourite colour — deep blue.

He went through to get his photos taken, smiling as he told them. 'This is a brilliant hoody.' He studied the colour. It appeared to be a single colour, deep sea blue, and yet...the depths of the colour was amazing.

'The colour is fantastic. I don't know how you've made it look so rich,' he said to Ethel.

'I use several similar shades of blue to spin the yarn,' Ethel explained. 'When they're all spun into a single strand of yarn and knitted up, it creates a depth of colour, that looks like a single tone, but is in fact different tones of blue.' She adjusted her shawl. 'I'm prattling on. I'm sure I'm boring you, Calum.'

'Not at all,' Calum said, and then he went to stand for the photos to be taken.

He wondered why everyone was smiling at him.

Aurora announced, 'The postmaster commissioned Ethel to knit the hoody for you as a gift.'

'Something to remind you of us,' the postmaster chimed–in. 'When you've gone back to your busy life in the city.'

Calum looked quite overcome. 'I intend coming back...one day.' He glanced at Emmie to gauge her reaction, and saw the emotion in her eyes. But several of the ladies were smiling, almost with happy tears, that his time with them was coming to an end. This was their time when they had a champion in their community. A time to remember with fond thoughts.

'I hope you do,' the postmaster said to him, but he was realistic enough to know that a young man's good intentions sometimes fade when he goes on to better things. Especially if Calum won his next fight. His fame was rising.

Calum went over and shook the postmaster's hand and gave him a manly hug. 'Thank you for the gift. I appreciate it.'

'I'm glad you like it, lad,' said the postmaster.

'Aurora, can you take a photo of us?' said Calum.

Aurora took a couple of pictures of Calum and the postmaster standing together, smiling. Then one of them posing, pretending to punch each other on the jaw. A fun shot.

'I'll give you copies,' Aurora promised both of them.

Calum whispered to Aurora. 'Could you put a picture of us in the magazine feature?'

Aurora grinned. 'Yes, as it's an online magazine. I can do that easily.'

'Don't tell the postmaster he's going to be in the magazine punching me in the chin.'

Aurora was happy to go along with the ruse. 'He won't know until it's published,' she whispered.

Calum and Aurora enjoyed a moment of playful scheming.

'Okay,' Aurora announced. 'There's just one more thing to do, and then we can let you run off, Calum.'

The carefully folded blue satin robe was passed from the back of the room and handed to Calum by Ethel.

'Another wee minding and a thank you for agreeing to the knitting feature,' said Ethel.

Calum accepted the gift, not knowing what it was until he unfolded it. He smiled and held it up. 'Thanks for making this. I love it.'

'Oh! We should get a group photo before you go,' said Aurora.

Everyone was up for this and stood together, with Calum in the middle, surrounded by the ladies. The postmaster stood beside Ethel with his arm around her shoulder.

Emmie stood beside Calum and as Aurora clicked the camera into action, a few of the shots captured him smiling down at Emmie.

Calum was still wearing the hoodie and flicked the hood up for effect.

Aurora instructed Emmie. 'Sort his hood for him, Emmie. So that it's sitting even and we can see his face, yet still have part in shadow.'

Emmie reached up and adjusted Calum's hood. He stood there, gazing at her as she fussed to get it right for the photos. Her heart fluttered, being so close to him, and seeing his green gaze focus on her.

At that moment, someone else walked into the living room.

'I knocked, but no one heard me,' said Hunter. Then he stared, taken aback, when he saw what appeared to be Emmie reaching up with her arms around Calum's neck to hug him.

Emmie was startled and jumped at the sound of Hunter's voice. Calum wrapped his strong arms around her preventing her from tumbling.

'Cosy night, eh?' Hunter remarked. No one missed the bitterness in his tone.

Emmie didn't know where she found the strength, but perhaps it was caused by the rotten boyfriends she'd had, and the way they often spoke to her, but she became defensive. 'It's a group photo for the magazine.' She said this, trying to keep her tone steady. But Hunter looked so handsome standing there wearing an open neck, cream linen shirt and dark trousers. Her heart reacted as it had done when she'd first seen him, and flashes of his toned body as he spoke to her through the car window, sent her senses alight. A blush burned across her cheeks and the effect he had on her was as potent as earlier.

'Hunter, come in,' Aurora said, waving to him. 'We've almost finished the knitting photos.'

'Maybe you could take one of all of us,' Emmie suggested boldly. 'Including Aurora.'

'Sure,' Hunter said, taking the camera from Aurora and handling it as if he was a pro.

Aurora stood beside Calum. He put his arms around her shoulder, and Emmie's shoulder, a gesture that made Hunter wish he was standing there instead.

Hunter clicked off a few shots. 'Would you like to change positions? Let another two ladies stand beside you.'

The women shuffled around and Ethel and Hilda now stood beside Calum. He put his arms around their shoulders and Hunter clicked another couple of shots. He checked the camera. 'These should work. Everyone is in the picture.'

Aurora came over and he handed the camera back to her.

'I'm so thrilled you could come along to the sewing bee night,' Aurora told Hunter. 'I didn't think you'd do it at such short notice.'

Hunter glanced at Emmie. When Aurora phoned him to ask if he'd be willing to be interviewed for a feature, she'd told him she was going to the sewing bee to take pictures for their knitting feature. He didn't know the model was Calum. All he knew was that Emmie was going to the sewing bee. This was all the incentive Hunter had needed.

CHAPTER SIX

Romance Brewing

'I'd better run,' Calum said, picking up the bag that Ethel had given to him containing his new hooded top and robe. He wanted to say something to Emmie before he left, but Hunter had monopolised her, so he settled for giving her a nod.

Emmie smiled at him and watched him leave. A pang of sadness washed over her.

The postmaster left with Calum and they walked along the esplanade. The sea air was warm without a breeze to cool the evening down.

'We're in for another scorching day I think,' the postmaster said, making light conversation as he sensed the heaviness in Calum's heart.

Calum agreed, and gazed out at the calm sea. Soon his time here would be over. He'd miss it. He'd miss everything. And he'd miss Emmie.

'I'll miss this when I leave,' Calum murmured.

'You could always come back, laddie.'

Calum nodded, but in his heart it felt like a lie.

He changed the subject. 'When are you going to ask Ethel to marry you?'

The postmaster smiled. 'I don't think it would suit her. Ethel likes her cottage, her business. I don't want to spoil things. We're happy with our kiss chase relationship.'

'You chase her and sometimes she lets you kiss her?'

'Something like that. Maybe one day we'll settle down. I've always loved Ethel, from the first time I ever saw her.'

Calum's heart was beating faster, the fighter in him starting to feel the adrenalin, the urge to go back to the sewing bee, to fight for Emmie. Then he gazed out at the sea and breathed in the calm night air.

They continued walking along, heading for the postmaster's house — a large house, a substantial piece of property.

'It's a shame the dressmaker doesn't go to the sewing bee,' Calum mused. 'She's missing out on all the fun those ladies have.'

'It's just her way.' He smiled thoughtfully. 'You seem to get on well with the dressmaker. Judith says they've practically adopted you.'

Calum laughed. 'They're lovely ladies. I like them. Their kindness is genuine. I feel I can drop my guard when I'm around them. But I wonder...is it true what they say about the dressmaker sewing magic into the dresses she makes?'

'She's definitely got the gift. I've known her for years. Her father used to work on the fishing boats down at the harbour, and the dressmaker would warn them when she sensed a storm was brewing. She was so reliable that eventually no one thought of it as being strange. If the dressmaker said there was going to be a storm, people started battening the hatches.'

'I get the feeling she can see right through me. And I think she knows the outcome of the fight.'

'She won't tell you.'

'I don't want her to,' Calum said firmly. 'Either way, I'd be going into the ring with prior knowledge. An unfair advantage. I've never cheated, because I'd only be cheating myself. That's never been my way.' He also figured that the dressmaker sensed how he felt about Emmie, and maybe she knew the outcome of that too. He didn't want to know that either. Romance would cloud his concentration. The last thing he needed was to fall in love. And it would be easy to fall for Emmie. He had to keep a clear head for the contest. Though Emmie would be difficult to forget.

The sewing bee ladies buzzed around Hunter asking questions about his books, while Aurora took photos of him. He'd brought copies of the first four books in his spy thriller series because Aurora had asked him if he could bring them along for the photos.

As the ladies gathered round for a final group picture, Hunter managed to whisper to Emmie. 'I need to talk to you about something, so don't disappear.' His eyes implored her to agree.

'Okay,' she whispered, wondering what it was that was so urgent.

'So you two are friends, eh?' said Hilda.

Emmie explained about being unable to find her way to the dressmaker's cottage and meeting Hunter. She omitted the parts about him being shirtless and the instant attraction she felt, but it was difficult to tell them without a blush giving them a clear hint of the effect Hunter had on her.

'Do you live in the forest?' Ione asked Hunter.

'No, I'm in one of the cottages on the edge of the forest.'

'Are you a hobby gardener?' Aurora asked him, taking notes to include in the feature. She'd already written the bulk of it, and as with Calum, she'd given Hunter the rough editorial for his approval.

'I don't have much time for any hobbies,' he said. 'The writing takes up a lot of my time, and when I'm not writing I'm doing book tours and promotions, and dealing with my publishers.'

'Success certainly seems to have a price for you,' Emmie remarked.

'At the moment, but I'm hoping that once this new book in the series is published I'll be able to write at a slower rate of knots.' His reply was general, to Emmie and the others listening, but then he added a personal note. 'I'm getting to a certain age when I'd like to consider settling down.' He glanced at Emmie.

'You're not married,' Aurora stated. 'According to recent interviews I've read about you.'

'No, I'm single,' he confirmed. 'But living in hope of meeting the right woman.'

Bea spoke up. 'Customers have been enjoying your books, your spy series. If this latest book is the final one in the series, do you have anything in mind for what you'll write? Another spy thriller series?'

'Definitely a thriller.' He didn't reveal any details.

'With romance in it,' said Bea. 'Readers comment that they love the romance in your novels.'

'I certainly do,' Judith told him. 'I feel like I'm in the story, that I get to know the characters, and the romances are wonderful. It's like watching a film. Your books would be perfect for making into films.'

'I'm actually in talks with my agent and publishers about that,' Hunter revealed.

'Can I mention this in the feature?' Aurora asked him. 'Or is it top secret?'

'You can mention it. This would be the first feature to discuss this, but I've had conference calls with my publishers while I've been at the cottage. There's definitely going to be a movie deal, though I can't give the details. The other thing that my agent is in discussions with is for a television series. A serialised thriller drama.'

The excitement rose throughout the sewing bee members, and Emmie was the first to ask him for more details.

'Would the series be based on your spy thrillers?' Emmie asked.

'No, this would be tied in with the new ideas I have. An eight part serialised series. One hour episodes.'

'Would you write the scripts?' said Emmie.

Hunter shrugged. 'I'd work with an established screenwriter, but I'd have a lot of input, and that's why I'm keen to get involved.'

'Would you be away to Hollywood?' Ione asked him.

'No. It would be filmed in studios down in England, and maybe in New York,' Hunter replied.

'This will be quite an exclusive story for our magazine,' Aurora said sounding excited.

'I phoned my agent before I drove here tonight, and he said that we need to get the publicity up and running. And you said that you'd let me confirm the details in the feature, so that's ideal.'

'Yes, I'll email it to you, and you can run it past your agent,' Aurora promised.

'With all the publicity and things you have to do, as well as writing your books, will you have time for romance?' Hilda asked him.

He sighed so hard that Emmie pictured the weight of this on his shoulders.

'I'll make time.' He glanced at Emmie as he said this, causing her to blush as the sewing bee ladies saw that he was directing his comment to her.

'I suppose the barbecue will be your first proper date with Emmie,' said Ione.

Emmie gasped.

'Yes, it will,' he said before Emmie could say anything. 'I hear it's going to be a fun night.'

'The summer barbecues are great fun,' Ethel told him. 'There's lots to eat, dancing and contests.'

Hunter frowned. 'Contests? What type?'

'Races, tug of war, sand skittles,' Ethel listed them off. 'You're a fit young man. You should compete. Though you'll need a partner for the three–legged race. I'm competing with the postmaster as my partner. You could team up with Emmie.'

'I haven't done the three–legged race since primary school,' said Emmie. 'I was rubbish at it. I never could get it right.'

'But you look fit, Emmie, and Hunter will power on and keep you right,' Ethel said helpfully.

Emmie stared at Hunter, hoping he'd veto the idea.

'I'm sure Emmie and I will give it a go, won't we?' He grinned at Emmie.

Everyone looked at her. She swallowed her reluctance and forced a smile. 'Oh, yes,' she lied.

'There's also the sack race and egg and spoon,' Ione added.

Emmie smiled tightly. 'A whole evening of fun then.'

'Calum could win the men's running event,' said Ione. 'With all that forest running. But you look fit too, Hunter. Do you go for runs in the forest? You look like you train.'

'I've been cycling and swimming,' he told Ione. 'I run along the shore some nights, but I haven't run in the forest.'

'I don't blame you. It's dark and scary in the forest at night.' Ione shuddered.

With her dinner date now looking more like a fiasco, Emmie wondered if she should've opted for dinner at a restaurant.

The chatter continued about Calum competing.

'Calum is involved in the barbecue cooking,' Ethel told them. 'Some of us will have to flip his sausages for him while he's competing.'

One of the ladies spoke up. 'I'm not running this year. I'd be happy to flip his bangers for him.'

'I'll volunteer too,' another member said. 'I prefer to watch the chaos rather than compete.'

Emmie's heart sank further with every comment.

'Cheer up, Emmie,' Hunter teased her. 'Even if we don't win, it's the fun of competing that matters.'

Emmie forced a smile. 'I can hardly wait.'

As Aurora took the last of the photos of Hunter, he handed Bea a handful of book templates. 'My publishers have these printed out and sent to me. I've signed them.'

Bea clasped the book templates. 'This is a brilliant idea. I can pop a signed template into some of your books.'

Hilda grabbed the quilt she'd brought along to the sewing bee to work on. She hadn't sewn a stitch, but she thrust it hopefully at Hunter. 'Would you sign my quilt for me?'

He was happy to oblige. *Hunter*, he wrote, using a pen Hilda gave him.

Hilda gazed at the name. 'I'll embroider this permanently on to the quilt.'

This caused numerous members to ask Hunter to sign their quilts and other items.

'I'm not an embroiderer,' one of the ladies said, gazing at his signature on her quilt. 'What type of stitch should I use to embroider Hunter's name?'

'A back stitch or stem stitch,' Emmie advised her.

'Emmie designs her own embroidery patterns,' Ethel reminded the ladies.

As the chatter circulated about embroidery stitches, Emmie thought that this would be Hunter's cue to leave. But instead, he accepted the offer of another cup of tea.

'Would you like a scone or a piece of shortbread with you tea?' offered Hilda.

'Yes, please,' he replied, causing the ladies to laugh.

The ladies wanted to see the embroidery that Emmie was working on. And the discussion led to them asking about the dresses she'd brought to the dressmaker.

'They're beautiful dresses,' said Emmie. 'The dressmaker designed them years ago.'

'Does anyone know about stitching secret messages into garments or knitted items, like a jumper?' Hunter asked them.

'Knitting in Morse code?' Ethel said to him.

Hunter nodded. 'I heard about messages being stitched in code, dots and dashes, recently.' He didn't reveal that he'd heard this regarding the dressmaker's designs.

Judith smiled over at him and gave him a nod, a thank you, for not telling them about the dressmaker's coded details.

Emmie kept this a secret too.

'Yes, I've heard of knitting messages on jumpers and cardigans,' Ethel confirmed. 'I haven't knitted them myself.'

For all the spy novels he'd written, and the research, this method of sending secret messages had eluded him. Now he was interested in incorporating this into his new book.

Hilda gave Hunter his tea, scone and shortbread, putting them down on the table beside him. 'Oh, you've got a button hanging by a thread,' she said, noticing it dangling from the top of his shirt collar. 'You'd better stitch it on secure.' She continued pouring tea for other members.

Hunter looked at Emmie.

'You want me to sew it on for you?' she offered.

'Would you? I could do it, but...sewing isn't my forte.'

Emmie opened her craft bag and pulled out her needle book where she kept a selection of needles for sewing and embroidery. A few were threaded ready to use.

'Will I have to take my shirt off?' he said.

The ladies reacted with giggles and smiles.

'No, I can stitch the button on without you taking it off,' said Emmie, and then began to stitch it on. Her hand touched his chest and she felt his strong, lean muscles. She was so close to him that she was sure he could hear the excited fluttering of her heart. His scent was fresh and clean with a hint of masculine aftershave.

Those beautiful blue eyes gazed at her as she stitched. She felt flustered, but not from the sewing. Every stitch made her realise that she was in jeopardy of falling for Hunter.

His deep voice sent her senses soaring. He murmured to her as she leaned close. 'I need to talk to you about the heroine in my first novel.' He flicked a glance at the books on the table beside him. The first novel sat on the top. 'There's something you should know.'

'What?'

'When I wrote her into the book, she was pure fiction. My ideal woman I suppose.'

'She sounds interesting, but what has that got to do with me?' She continued stitching.

'When you read how I've described her, I think you'll understand.' His gaze penetrated deep into her eyes. 'I've described a character that's like you.'

65

Her eyes widened. 'Your heroine looks like me?'

He nodded and whispered. 'I think that's why I can't stop thinking about you since I met you.'

'What are you two whispering about?' Hilda said, interrupting the moment.

Several members smiled at them.

Emmie blushed, realising that they'd been so deep in whispers they hadn't noticed that the ladies were watching them and reading them like a book.

'I think we've got a wee romance brewing,' Ethel whispered to Aurora.

Aurora nodded. 'But where does that leave Calum? It's obvious he likes Emmie too.'

Ethel shrugged and adjusted the shawl around her shoulders. 'I don't know, but Hunter's definitely interested in her.'

Emmie finished sewing the button on. 'There, that's it sorted.' She put the needle back in her needle book.

One of the ladies came over to Emmie holding her quilt that Hunter had signed. 'I enjoy quilting, but my embroidery is messy. Would you mind helping me embroider Hunter's signature? I don't want it to fade.'

Emmie was happy to help and used strands of floss to embroider his name on the quilt using back stitches. The blue thread matched the aqua tones of the quilt.

Hunter drank his tea and ate his scone and shortbread while the chatter swept around him. He listened to Emmie describe in more detail the dressmaker's designs.

'What type of fabric were the dressmaker's original dresses made from?' Ione asked her. 'Were they prints or solid colours?'

'Prints. Beautiful florals and polka dots. One of the dresses had a lily of the valley print and I really loved it.'

'So you're going to be staying here to help the dressmaker with the designs for the television series?' Bea asked Emmie.

'I am. I'm flattered and excited,' said Emmie. 'I've done dressmaking, lots of alternations to clothes, especially dresses, for years. I love to upscale vintage dresses, but working with the dressmaker this afternoon was amazing. Her pattern books are filled with original sketches.'

'I love fashion illustrations,' said Aurora. 'Do you think the dressmaker would be willing to let us show a couple of them in the magazine?'

'I'll ask her,' Judith promised. 'She has sketch books full of them.'

The evening continued with sewing, embroidery, knitting, tea and chatter.

Finally, the sewing bee night was over and the ladies started heading home.

'I'll see you in the morning,' Judith said to Emmie. 'Pop up after breakfast. The dressmaker starts work early.'

'I'm looking forward to it,' Emmie said, smiling. She picked up her craft bag that was now stuffed with the sample bag of yarn from Ethel.

Hunter bid the ladies goodnight and followed Emmie out into the calm night.

'Can I give you a lift to your cottage?' he said.

'It's not far, I can walk.'

'Come on,' he encouraged her. 'And I wanted to give you this.' He held up the first book in his series. 'Read it when you have time. Let me know if you think the character reminds you of yourself.'

Emmie went to accept the book, but he smiled at her and held on to it. 'It's quite heavy and with all that yarn in your bag, it'll be awkward to carry.' He motioned to his car parked nearby.

'Okay,' she said, feeling flutters of excitement as she got into his black sports car. It was stylish and luxurious, and felt so intimate when he sat beside her, started up the engine and drove off along the esplanade.

Emmie looked at the sea glistening as they drove the short distance to her cottage. For a moment she glimpsed what her life would be like if she became involved with Hunter.

'I enjoyed myself at the sewing bee,' he told her.

'It's the first time I've ever been to one. I know it was a bit different because Aurora wanted to take photos for the magazine. But I'm glad I've joined them. Ethel says it's on once or twice a week.'

'You'll get plenty of sewing done. And you'll be working with the dressmaker.'

'A dream job. What an opportunity.'

By now they'd reached her cottage and Hunter pulled up outside. 'I'll pick you up tomorrow night for the barbecue.'

Emmie smiled. 'Remember to wear something you can run in.'

Hunter laughed. 'I'd forgotten about the three–legged race. Are you really rubbish at it?'

'Totally.'

He smiled at her. 'Okay, so we're not going to win that one. What about the sack race?'

Emmie bit her lip.

'I'm not sensing much confidence for that one either.'

'Noooo.'

'Egg and spoon?'

'Hmmm.'

They both laughed.

'It promises to be an interesting night. Maybe I should just book us a table for dinner at the local restaurant.'

'I'd thought about that too,' she confessed.

'But it wouldn't be as challenging.'

'Or as much fun.'

'The barbecue it is then,' he said firmly.

'See you tomorrow night, Hunter.' Emmie got out of the car.

'Don't forget the book.' He handed it to her.

'Is she really like me? I mean, I design embroidery patterns and sew dresses. Not really a character from a spy novel.'

'It's her physical description that has an uncanny likeness to you. And her attitude.'

'Stubborn?'

He shrugged and smiled.

'I'll read the book.' She walked away, smiling to herself as Hunter waved and drove off.

What a night it had been. She sighed, put her bag and the book down, flicked on the lamps, kicked her shoes off and padded through to the kitchen to make a cup of tea before falling into bed. An early start in the morning. She needed to get some sleep.

But as she lay in bed, gazing out the window at the night sky, she kept thinking about Hunter...and Calum...

The postmaster stood at his kitchen door, sipping a cup of tea, watching Calum hit the punch bag that was hanging up in the garden. Two lanterns lit up the garden at night and the light from the kitchen cast a glow across the lawn. The figure of Calum, wearing his dark training gear and boxing gloves, looked like a shadow, punching the bag relentlessly.

Calum stopped, steadied the bag and glanced round at the postmaster. 'Put your gloves on.' His words sounded clear in the warm night air.

The postmaster frowned. 'My boxing gloves?'

Calum nodded and motioned for him to go and get them. 'You've only got three or four pairs. The ones hanging in the hall. The pair in the living room...'

'Okay, I'll be back in a minute.'

Calum put his hands on his hips and breathed deeply while he waited, calming his heart rate.

The postmaster emerged a few minutes later, tightening the wrist straps on the gloves, a new pair that he'd barely broken in. He'd put his boots on too, the ones he'd had for years. They were well worn, but saw very little action since his days in the ring. He'd kept them, a reminder of what he used to be.

'You've got the boots too, eh?' Calum said, smiling.

'I've also got my boxing shorts, but I decided not to wear them. It would give me an unfair advantage.'

'How so?'

'Because if you saw my chicken legs in my shorts, you wouldn't be able to stop laughing. I'd knock you for six while you were snickering.'

Calum laughed.

'I used to have muscled legs from all my training and running when I was your age. Now as a postmaster, I only dart around organising parcels and deliveries. I've no time for training.'

'Except for running after Ethel.'

'Yes, there's that.'

Calum glanced at the gloves. 'They look like new.'

The postmaster nodded. 'Ethel gave them to me for my birthday.' He finished tightening them to fit his wrists.

'Ethel made your dressing gown, and your kitchen curtains. She does a lot for you.'

'She does.' His acknowledgment sounded deep, thoughtful, in the calm night. He walked towards Calum. He got the message.

Ethel did a lot for him. He should consider marrying her. He changed the focus to Calum. 'Did you see Emmie when you were running to exhaustion back and forth along the esplanade?'

Calum didn't deny he'd done this. Unable to settle, he'd gone for a run along the esplanade, keeping an eye on Ethel's cottage, wondering when the sewing bee night would finish. He hoped he'd see Emmie, and he did. 'Hunter gave her a lift in his car to her cottage.'

'Any smooching?'

'Not that I saw.' His heart had twisted seeing Hunter with Emmie.

'Maybe you should chase her, like I run after Ethel?'

Calum smiled. 'What? And end up with chicken legs like yours? No thank you.'

Poking fun at each other, they got ready to spar.

'Go one round with me,' said Calum. 'Then we'll call it a night.'

'Remember, I've got work to do in the morning, so don't go giving me a black eye.'

'Just a wee bit of light sparring. Nobody will get hurt.'

They squared up to each other in the middle of the lawn in the large garden, lit by the glow of the lantern lights, with the vast night sky arching above them.

Calum pretended to ring the starter bell. 'Ding! Ding!'

And off they went, with the postmaster throwing a couple of left hooks at Calum.

'A southpaw, eh?' Calum smiled as he bobbed and weaved, and issued a jab at the postmaster who deftly countered with an attempted uppercut to Calum's chin. 'Oh, nice one. You've got some tidy moves there,' Calum complimented him, seeing the years of training from his opponent's past.

Their laughter and cheers rang clear, filtering into the night air for the three minutes of their boxing match. Neither of them struck any heavy blows on the other, and the postmaster enjoyed going the distance with the young champ. Happy memories made for both of them.

CHAPTER SEVEN

Dressmaker Designs

Emmie was up early, eager to start working on the dressmaker's designs.

After a breakfast of cereal with fresh strawberries and a cup of tea, she put on a light blue chambray dress, packed her craft bag, picked up the sketch book of fashion illustrations, Hunter's book, and drove up to the dressmaker's cottage.

A heat haze lingered over the landscape, and she drove with the windows open, breathing in the sea air, then the scent of the forest. Sunlight flickered through the trees as she headed deeper into the forest and parked outside the cottage. The front door was open and she rang the doorbell and ventured in, hearing the sound of Judith's chatter drifting through to the hall from the living room.

'Morning,' Judith said cheerily seeing Emmie walk in.

'It feels like it's going to be another scorcher,' Emmie said, putting her bag down and eyeing the freshly brewed pot of tea on the table.

'Help yourself to a cuppa,' Judith told Emmie.

Emmie poured a cup of tea while the dressmaker stood in front of one of the walls of fabric, selecting the fabrics for the dresses they would be working on. Heavier fabrics such as brocades and velvet were stacked on the lower shelves, while bolts of satin and cotton and linen with ditsy prints and polka dots filled the middle shelves. Silks, organza, georgette and chiffon were tucked on the top shelves, mainly within easy reach, but a sturdy step ladder was propped up nearby.

'I brought your sketch book back.' Emmie put it down on the table. 'I haven't had a chance to study it all, but I love the designs for the evening dresses.'

'The production company are happy with the dresses I've sent to them so far,' the dressmaker explained.

'Will you have to go down to the studios in England to fit the dresses personally?' Emmie asked her.

'No, they have wardrobe staff to make any alterations,' said the dressmaker. 'I've been given the exact measurements, but obviously some of the dresses will need slight adjustments, though apparently the fit has been great so far.' She lifted a roll of eau de nil satin from a shelf. 'This satin drapes beautifully and we're blending it with a sea foam silk chiffon.'

Judith lifted down a roll of velvet and carried it through to the sewing room.

The dressmaker followed her carrying the satin.

Emmie went to help the dressmaker, but she was quite capable of carrying it herself.

'Could you bring through the sea foam chiffon,' the dressmaker said to Emmie. 'It's marked with a label on the shelf above the printed cotton.'

Emmie lifted the chiffon from the shelf and sat it down on the cutting table in the sewing room.

'As we have to work to a tight deadline,' the dressmaker began, 'I won't take time to explain the details of the fabrics. We'll get all the pattern pieces cut this morning. Then have lunch, and sew the dresses with the minimum of fuss.'

'Are we making evening dresses?' Emmie asked, helping the dressmaker unroll the satin and fold it ready for cutting. Pattern pieces were to be pinned on.

'One of them is a full–length satin and chiffon evening dress and it'll be worn for a party scene where the character will be dancing. So we'll have to take into consideration the drape, the movement. Create a beautiful dress for one of the main romantic scenes.' The dressmaker showed Emmie the illustration she'd drawn that depicted the dress.

'It's gorgeous.'

'We need to consider the sound aspect,' the dressmaker explained. 'Some fabrics are beautiful, but they rustle when they're worn and the sound could be picked up during filming.'

Emmie nodded. 'I had a taffeta dress and I loved the sound the fabric made when I swished the skirt around, but I appreciate this wouldn't be ideal when there are microphones around.'

'Exactly.' The dressmaker showed her another design. 'The other is a classy velvet dress. There are a lot of dramatic moments in the series and the production company want to use the costumes to help promote the series. They're a big part of the overall theme.'

'What is the main theme?' asked Emmie.

'Rich, influential people whose lives are intertwined with love and loss,' said the dressmaker. 'Love lost, hearts broken and eventually mended through meeting new acquaintances, but all within this exciting drama.'

'That does sound dramatic,' said Emmie, studying the fashion illustrations and feeling like she already sensed the high quality of the production.

'The colours play a large role in creating a sense of the past, but the recent past. We're not talking about this as a period piece.' The dressmaker indicated the information that was on the screen of her laptop nearby. 'These are pictures of the set designs. We need to create dresses that look like they belong in that world, while being outstanding to highlight the leading ladies.'

'It's quite a complicated process,' Emmie acknowledged.

'I've been working on it for months.'

'Have you met any of the cast?' said Emmie.

'Only via online conference calls,' the dressmaker explained. 'Their exact measurements were sent to me initially so that I could start on the designs. The company's production notes were flexible, but I like to be able to have a free hand to create designs like these.'

'All the dressmaker needs is the exact measurements of the stars,' said Judith. 'Then she works on the designs. She gets to read the script and coordinate the costumes with the set designer and showrunner.'

'The previous television series I designed for had a different process entirely,' the dressmaker explained to Emmie. 'So we need to be flexible in our methods. But I like the atmosphere of this new series — interesting characters with plenty of drama and romance.'

'They've included a few dance scenes when the main characters go to parties.' Judith sounded enthusiastic. 'So a couple of extra special full–length dresses were needed. The dressmaker made them and sent them to the studio and they love them. I loved them too. One had layers of chiffon with a sprinkling of sparkle and the other was white georgette shot through with silver thread.'

Emmie smoothed the fabric and folded it ready for the paper pattern pieces to be pinned on and cut ready for sewing while they chatted. 'When you're designing a dress, do you create the design and then select the fabric?' she asked the dressmaker.

'It depends. Sometimes the fabric leads to the design. I have suppliers who keep an eye out for wonderful fabric.'

'Remember that sparkling scarlet fabric?' said Judith. 'You made it into a cocktail dress that made me wish I had the nerve to wear something like that. But I'm more your pastel and neutral tones type. I've never actually worn a daring red cocktail number. It was a dazzler.'

'I loved that fabric,' the dressmaker agreed. 'That was one fabric that led the design process. I knew as soon as the bolt of it was delivered that it had to be cocktail dress.'

Judith smiled as she pictured it. 'That was a dress with a hot night guarantee.'

Emmie laughed.

'It's true,' Judith insisted, smiling.

'Maybe one day you'll be bold and wear a little red party dress,' Emmie said to Judith.

'In my dreams,' Judith replied.

'It's nice to dream though, isn't it?' the dressmaker mused.

They all agreed.

'What type of evening dress would you go for?' Judith asked Emmie.

'I've never worn a red evening dress either. I love light sea blues, turquoise, and pastel tones. And white and gold. I like silver, but it doesn't suit me.'

The dressmaker nodded. 'Silver and gold would be my dream selection, but I usually stick to pale blue, lilac and beige.'

'What are you wearing for your date tonight with Hunter?' Judith asked Emmie.

'Not a dress. If I'm running while tied to Hunter, I'm thinking something I can race in.'

Judith laughed. 'I suppose there are worse things than being tied to Hunter for your first date.'

Emmie blushed, but she tended to agree.

'Did Hunter give you a wee kiss last night?' Judith asked Emmie.

Emmie blinked. 'No. But he gave me a copy of one of his books.' She told them about her reminding Hunter of his leading lady character.

'You remind him of a character from one of his books?' Judith was taken aback.

'Apparently. He wants me to read the book and see if I recognise myself in the story. It's the first book in the series. The character doesn't end up dating the leading man at the end of the story, but he's planning to make a comeback for her in his new book.'

Judith carried the rolls of fabric back through to the living room and stacked them on the shelves after the pattern pieces had been cut. 'I've read all the books in his series, and I remember that character. I liked her.'

'Do you think she looked like Emmie?' the dressmaker asked Judith.

Judith walked back into the sewing room and studied Emmie. 'Yes, I had a picture of her in my mind, from the description Hunter had written. I suppose he's got an even clearer image of what that character looks like — and it seems she's like you, Emmie.'

'I don't know if that's a good thing or not,' said Emmie, as she helped the dressmaker with the paper pattern pieces.

The dressmaker worked efficiently and pinned each piece on the fabric ready for Emmie to cut. 'Hunter described her as his ideal woman. I think I'd take this as a compliment. You'll find out this evening at the barbecue whether you get along well or not.'

Emmie bit her lip as she unhooked a pair of scissors from the rack and started to cut around the pattern pieces. 'I don't want to get involved in a summer fling and have my heart broken.'

'You can take your time, get to know him,' said the dressmaker.

'But I don't see how I fit into Hunter's world.'

'Love is never easy,' the dressmaker told Emmie. 'Relax and have fun, but keep your guard up too. It's a fine balance.'

Emmie sighed heavily. 'Here I am sounding as if I'm complaining about having a date with Hunter. Lots of women would jump at the chance to date him.'

'Wait until you see him make a total eejit of himself in the sack,' Judith said, selecting yarn from her stash ready to start knitting.

Emmie blinked.

Judith quickly corrected herself. 'In the sack race. I wasn't meaning...' She giggled.

Their laughter lightened the mood, and they worked diligently to get lots of sewing done before lunch.

'What was it like to go to the movie premiere in London?' Emmie asked them. 'I read that it was ultra glamorous.'

'It was,' the dressmaker confirmed, machining the eau de nil satin and sea foam chiffon dress.

'But so were we,' Judith chimed-in. 'We were well–dressed, wearing clothes designed by the dressmaker, so I felt confident with that, but I was more starstruck than I thought I'd be. We had a great time.'

The dressmaker agreed. 'The celebrity scene isn't something I'd want to be part of regularly, but it was fascinating to attend a few of the functions. We'll no doubt get involved in events with this new television series when it launches. And other invitations still pop up in my emails too.' She shrugged. 'So you never know, we may attend some more.'

'We'd need to get our hair done again.' Judith flicked her salt and pepper curls. 'Ione did our hair for us. She does hair colouring on the side, as well as making her fairy dolls. I had my glitter strands blonded, and the dressmaker became her original blonde bombshell.'

The dressmaker laughed. 'Ione encouraged us to go for the full glamorous look. I rather liked it.'

'Maybe we'll get our hair done again this summer anyway,' said Judith, casting on her first row of stitches.

'What are you knitting?' Emmie looked at the white and gold mix yarn that Judith was using.

'A tippet. A type of stole, like a scarf, worn around the shoulders. I've knitted two and this is the last one I need to make. Tippets are worn with the evening dresses. They knit up easy and tie with a velvet ribbon. This is the pattern.'

Emmie admired the picture of the knitted tippet. 'The yarn you're using is lovely.'

'It's from Ethel's collection. She spun the sparkly gold thread into the white yarn,' Judith explained. 'The tippets knit up lovely in lace weight and double knitting yarns too. I'll give you a copy of the pattern. You could knit one up in an evening.'

Emmie nodded, thinking about the samples of yarn Ethel had given her at the sewing bee. She had the urge to knit something with it and a tippet would be perfect.

'This tippet is to go with the gold cocktail dress on the mannequin,' Judith told Emmie.

Two mannequins stood near the window where the natural light poured in. One had a calico toile draped and pinned on it, a new design the dressmaker was making. The other had a finished dress, a beautiful gold cocktail length dress. Gold sequins and embroidery embellished the design. The dressmaker had been working on it the previous night.

'This is fantastic,' Emmie enthused, studying the dress. 'I love the sequins and embroidery.' She imagined it would sparkle and shimmer when it was worn.

'It's almost finished. It's one that I was working on last night.' The dressmaker paused. 'Maybe you could finish the embroidery for me.'

'I'd be glad to.' Emmie saw that the embroidery pattern had been marked on the fabric — flowers and leaves.

'The embroidery thread is beside the mannequin. I used two strands of gold coloured threads. I'm sure you can see the pattern.'

Emmie couldn't wait to work on it. 'Is it okay if I use my own needles?'

'Yes, whatever works for you.'

Emmie set about embroidering the flowers using satin stitch and French knots, using one of her favourite needles from her needle book. Then she finished embroidering the leaves with closed fly stitch. She was used to working efficiently, so it didn't take long to embroider a few flowers and leaves.

'Beautiful work, Emmie,' said the dressmaker. 'It makes such a difference to have an expert embroiderer helping us.'

The first half of the morning was a blur of activity and chatter in the sewing room. Emmie was impressed by the efficiency of the dressmaker as she sat at her sewing machine, stitching the satin and chiffon dress. She worked fast, and Emmie felt she'd learned a lot from watching her techniques, especially the way she finished the edges of her seams using an overlocker, and machined narrow hems on the chiffon.

'Can you use an overlocker, Emmie?' the dressmaker asked her.

'Yes, do you want me to finish the seams?'

'It would let me get one of the dresses I was working on last night finished in time for the courier picking it up.'

While Emmie overlocked the seams, the dressmaker finished stitching an evening dress that had a velvet bodice and chiffon skirt made from several layers of fabric in shades of bronze and gold.

Judith parcelled up the dress, and after it was picked up by the courier to be sent off for fitting and approval, they had lunch outside on the patio.

They sat in the shade under a turquoise blue garden umbrella enjoying vegetable soup sprinkled with chives and served with salad and fresh crusty bread. Judith had made the soup, and she'd baked a lemon cake iced with frosting and decorated with slices of crystallised lemon.

Emmie bit into a slice of the cake with the melt in the mouth frosting. She nodded her delight to Judith.

The dressmaker sipped her tea. 'Judith phoned me last night after the sewing bee to tell me that Aurora wants to include a couple of my fashion sketches in the magazine. I had a look through my sketch books and I found the original drawings of the dresses you brought here.'

Emmie's eyes widened. 'You have the original artwork for those dresses? After all these years?'

'I keep everything.' The dressmaker shrugged. 'Anyway, I phoned Aurora this morning and she wants to expand on the feature — include that you bought the dresses and brought them here to me, and now you're working here for the summer. Are you up for this? Aurora would interview you and you'd be part of the feature. And she says she'd tie in your embroidery patterns to the feature following it.'

Emmie nodded enthusiastically. 'I'd definitely be up for this.'

'It would be a lovely feature,' Judith said happily. 'It'll show the original pen and ink sketches and the original dresses as they are now.'

'Aurora is coming here to photograph the dresses,' the dressmaker told Emmie.

The excitement of being featured with the dressmaker herself made Emmie smile.

'I'll make us another pot of tea.' Judith picked up the teapot and went through to the kitchen while Emmie and the dressmaker finished their cake.

'Do you have Hunter's book with you? The one he gave you last night?' the dressmaker asked.

Emmie dug it out of her craft bag, and they sat in the hot sunshine skimming through the pages until they came to the description of the leading lady.

It was clear from Emmie's expression when she read it that the character did sound like her.

Judith carried through the tea and set it down. 'I see you're reading Hunter's book. Have you found the bit you were looking for? I sort of remember what she was like.'

'Hunter was telling the truth,' said Emmie. 'It's like reading about myself, though I don't know what the character does for a living in the story.'

'She's a fashion photographer,' Judith told her. 'She inadvertently photographs something that happens in one of the action–packed fight scenes, and that's how she comes to be involved in the story — and ends up having a romance with the leading man.'

'But they don't stay together at the end.' Emmie wanted to clarify what happened.

'No, she goes back to her own life and he continues with his secret agent assignments,' Judith explained.

'I wonder what Hunter will do to bring her back into the storyline for his new book?' the dressmaker mused.

'Maybe they'll meet by chance,' Judith suggested. 'And have a hot summer romance,' she added.

They smiled and agreed that a sizzling romance could be part of Emmie's summer, beginning with the barbecue night that promised to be a scorcher in itself.

CHAPTER EIGHT

A Sizzling Hot Night

'Did you hear someone shout?' Judith asked Emmie and the dressmaker as they finished their lunch outside in the garden.

Emmie ate the last piece of her lemon cake. She paused to listen. Nothing except the sound of the bees buzzing around the edge of the garden where it merged with the forest. 'I didn't hear anyone.'

Neither did the dressmaker, but she sensed something, especially when Thimble became alert and prowled across the garden.

Still silence.

Then the sound of a woman's voice shouting something unclear, followed by silence again.

The ladies looked at each other, and then the three of them hurried inside and through to the hallway. The front door was still wedged open from earlier.

'One more time,' a woman shouted from nearby.

Peering outside they saw it was Aurora shouting instructions to Calum.

Judith frowned at the dressmaker and Emmie. 'Whatever is she doing? She's got Calum running around those trees like a hobby horse on a carnival ride.'

He wore a boxer's grey vest that emphasised his muscled shoulders, black training trousers, running shoes — and a slightly harassed expression.

'Aurora!' the dressmaker called to her.

She glanced round at the sound of her name. 'I'll be there in a minute.' She smiled and continued encouraging Calum to sprint through the forest while she captured it on her phone. She checked the playback and shouted to him. 'Thank you, Calum. I've got what I need.'

He came bounding over to Aurora and waved to the ladies, delighted when he saw that Emmie was there.

'What are you up to?' Judith called to Aurora.

She hurried over, eager to show the ladies what she'd filmed for the magazine's website. 'I was driving up to your cottage to take the pictures of the vintage dresses when I saw Calum out for a run. We've got photos of him from last night at the sewing bee, but nothing outdoors to depict his training here in the forest. So, when I saw him I thought I'd ask him to run around, as if he was training, while I filmed him with my phone.' She held her phone up to show them. 'Doesn't he look great. We've got an original piece of footage. I was going to use clips from his website, but now we've got our own clip.'

The dressmaker's voice sounded calm. 'Would you like a drink of water before you continue with your run, Calum?'

'I wouldn't mind,' he said, smiling. He wasn't exhausted by any means, just slightly put off his stride by Aurora's insistence that he leap over the gnarled tree roots while running as fast as he could. And smile. Then run towards the camera looking intense. That's all she wanted. It would only take a few minutes, but somehow it felt longer.

He smiled at Emmie as they all headed into the cottage and through to the back garden.

'I hope I'm not disturbing your lunch,' he said, seeing the table set and the remnants of cake and tea.

'We'd just finished,' the dressmaker assured him.

'Here you go, Calum.' Judith hurried through from the kitchen and handed him a refreshing glass of water.

'Thanks, Judith,' he said, and then smiled at Emmie. 'How's the dressmaking going?'

'We've been busy all morning,' Emmie told him. 'The dresses are wonderful. I've been cutting the patterns and finishing some embroidery.' She stopped, wondering if she was prattling, but he seemed interested to hear what she'd been up to.

'I won't hang around too long,' Aurora assured them. 'I thought I'd take the photos of the dresses — and get a copy of your original sketches.'

'The dresses are hanging up in the living room.' The dressmaker led Aurora inside and over to a walk–in cupboard that Emmie hadn't even known existed. It was build into one of the walls, and opened up, like a secret vault that was filled with rails of fabulous dresses.

Aurora wasn't surprised, so Emmie assumed she'd seen it before, but Emmie couldn't help comment when she peeked inside. 'Wow! Look at all those dresses!'

'You should see the other two cupboards in the spare room,' Judith told Emmie. 'Step inside any of them and be prepared to be mesmerised.'

Emmie was already mesmerised looking at the dresses in the cupboard in front of her.

Calum joined them and peered over Emmie's shoulder, towering above her. He had the sense to put his glass of water down and bring it nowhere near the cupboard.

Emmie stood gazing into the cupboard, wanting to step inside and have a rummage through the rails.

Torn between leaving them to it, and yet reluctant to forgo spending a bit of time with Emmie, Calum hesitated.

'I know you're training,' Judith said to him. 'But have you had your lunch? Would you like a wee bowl of vegetable soup? We've salad and lemon cake too. Home made.'

His stomach rumbled at the thought of it. He hadn't eaten anything except a protein drink for breakfast. He'd planned his day differently, but things went awry when the postmaster, extra busy at the post office, asked him to help set up the stalls and equipment for the barbecue. A lot needed to be assembled, and apparently it was an all–day task with several people, including some of the strong farmers, setting it all up. Then he'd decided to go for a run before lunch. That plan would've worked if he had been waylaid by Aurora. So here he was. He'd been running around all morning, one way or another, and feeling hungry. With his level of intense training he burned up everything he consumed so fast.

Judith smiled her encouragement to him.

'I don't want to impose on you again,' he said.

'Nonsense.' Judith brushed his concern aside and ushered him through to sit down at the table in the garden. 'Soup and salad coming right up.' And off she went, scurrying through to the kitchen, happy to make him some lunch.

Meanwhile, Aurora was taking photographs of the dresses. 'It must be strange to see them again after all these years,' she commented to the dressmaker.

'It is, especially as they're in such lovely condition. Emmie was kind enough to wash them and brought them here so they didn't get lost in the post.'

Aurora smiled at Emmie, and then continued to snap pictures of the dresses, including close–ups of the fabric.

The dressmaker and Emmie exchanged a worried look wondering if Aurora would notice the dots and dashes, but this seemed to bypass her totally, so neither of them highlighted this added little aspect.

'I don't suppose you could put the dresses on,' Aurora began. She lifted one of the tea dresses up and eyed Emmie. 'You'd fit into this easily.' Then she picked up the polka dot dress, the one the dressmaker loved so much. 'And you'd suit this so well...'

Judith served up a tasty lunch for Calum, and Thimble sat in the sunshine keeping him company while he ate it. In the background he could hear the women's voices chattering and a lot of giggling going on. But he left them to it and enjoyed his soup, salad and bread.

By the time Judith had dealt with Calum, the dressmaker and Emmie were standing in the living room wearing the dresses. Judith gasped and stopped in her tracks. For a moment she felt a wave of emotion, of sheer delight, seeing the dressmaker wearing the polka dot design. 'After all these years...' she murmured. Her long–time friend looked as she remembered her from her earlier years.

The dressmaker nodded and clearly she was feeling quite emotional too. She hid it well, but Judith saw the effect it had on her.

Aurora started to direct them to stand in front of the shelves of fabric.

The dressmaker held up her hand. 'I never include pictures of my living room or my sewing room, Aurora. We can take the photos outside in the garden. I don't mind people seeing that.'

Aurora was about to comply, understanding the dressmaker liking her privacy, but it was Calum's comment that made the dressmaker reconsider.

'What a pity,' he said. 'This is one of the most incredible rooms I've ever seen. Walls of fabric. It's like a living work of art.'

The women paused, taken aback, unsure what to do.

Calum continued. 'If you want to keep it a secret, fine, but if you stood in front of the wall of fabric, that's all people would see. They wouldn't see the whole room.'

The dressmaker blinked, as if a spark of realisation had dawned her. 'Could you do that, Aurora?'

'Definitely. Stand there, close the cupboard door and move the wee table and stepladder aside.'

Calum lifted them carefully out of the way, while Judith closed the cupboard door.

'Perfect.' Aurora made sure she had them both in the picture, snapped a few shots, and then repeated this with each of them individually. 'These pictures will be amazing. Good suggestion, Calum.'

Judith was still a bit flustered. She'd never have thought that the dressmaker would've agreed to this. Then she glanced at Calum. His straightforward suggestion was exactly what had been needed.

Emmie smiled when she saw that Thimble had somehow been captured in one of the photos, tucked in close, sitting beside the dressmaker as she stood in front of the fabulous coloured fabrics. 'This is my favourite.'

Aurora scrolled through the images and saw that Thimble was in one other photo that included Emmie standing beside the dressmaker while the cat sat at the dressmaker's side. 'This is my favourite. Look at those dresses. The fabric, the colours, and the cat. What a magical picture. The lead pic for the feature.'

Judith made tea for everyone, and Aurora joined them outside for a cuppa and a slice of lemon cake.

'I need the recipe for your lemon cake, Judith,' Calum said to her.

'I'll give you a copy,' she said, smiling happily.

Later, when Emmie arrived back at strawberry jam cottage, it was those moments she recalled. Calum had stayed a while, chatting, enjoying the company, and then headed out for his run. 'I'll see you at the barbecue, Emmie.' He'd waved to her and then disappeared into the depths of the forest, running off into the distance.

And she pictured the dressmaker, wearing one of her original designs. It felt like the past and the present had overlapped.

Emmie wondered if she had a future here after all. But the second she thought this, a low rumble sounded, like thunder over the sea, threatening a storm. She hurried over to the window and gazed out at the clear blue sky. No hint of clouds, no storm.

Taking a deep breath, she started to get ready for her date with Hunter. The time had flown in. He'd be here to pick her up in less than half an hour. Time to jump in the shower and then decide what to wear for a lively night of fun and contests.

Emmie saw Hunter's car pull up outside her cottage. The pretty butterfly print on her white summery cotton top with its sweetheart neckline and short puff sleeves seemed appropriate for her mood — the butterflies of excitement were fluttering through her at the thought of her first date with Hunter.

She watched him step out of the car, all beige and neutral tones — classy trousers, open neck shirt and training shoes. His look was expensive casual. Her slim–fitting, cream trousers and lace up deck shoes toned in with his attire. She wore her hair tied back in a tidy ponytail. They looked like a well–matched couple. But even the thought of the word *couple* made her nervous. Was she seriously contemplating this? She shrugged her doubts aside and watched him approach.

His hair was swept back from his handsome face, but a few strands had a tendency to fall sexily over his forehead and refused to be tamed. Would Hunter? Would she?

Taking a steadying breath, she hurried to the door and opened it casually, smiling as if she wasn't feeling giddy with glee. Maybe she could run off all her nervous energy in the races. Perhaps they had a chance of placing in the top three of the three–legged race after all.

'Ready to have fun?' he said, giving her a smile that set her senses on fire.

Was. She. Ever.

The esplanade was busy with people heading down on to the sand where the barbecue was set up. Various stalls and stands were dishing up everything from baked potatoes to cheeseburgers piled with salad and relish. Grills were sizzling with tasty delights, and the warm evening air was filled with the aroma of the barbecue food.

'They've really gone all out to provide a great summer barbecue party,' said Hunter.

Emmie felt the excitement in the air, and as they walked across the esplanade, leaving Hunter's car parked outside her cottage, she gazed out at the shimmering sea. The evening still retained a substantial amount of the day's heat, and she was glad she'd worn cool cotton and tied her hair back. She blinked against the fading sun glinting off the sea, scanning the people, searching for faces she recognised. The first one she saw was Calum. He was looking up at her from the shore where he manned one of the barbecue grills, and was deftly cooking and serving up burgers alongside the postmaster who ensured that Calum's buns were split and in ready supply.

The main walkway down on to the shore was crowded, so Hunter decided to take a quicker route down. 'Come on, Emmie, let's jump the wall.' He jumped down from the wall on the esplanade on to the sand.

Emmie hesitated.

Hunter's outstretched arms beckoned her. 'It's not that high. I'll catch you.'

Feeling a few eyes on her, wondering if she'd have the nerve to go for it, that stubborn streak in her helped give her the daring edge she needed.

Emmie jumped, trusting that Hunter would catch her, and if he didn't, it really wasn't that high, and all she'd risk was a dose of embarrassment and a soft landing in the sand.

Hunter caught her with more ease than she'd anticipated. In fact, he held her up in his strong arms, smiling gleefully, swung her around as if she was light as a patchwork doll, and then he put her gently down.

He towered over her, giving her a dazzling smile. He looked like he'd caught some of the sun from working in his garden, and the light bronze glow highlighted his handsome features.

His hands were still on her waist, holding her while he had an excuse to do so, and her heart reacted to his strength and potent masculinity. Hopefully, he'd attribute her blush to the effects of the sun on her face, rather than the roaring beat of her heart as her senses ignited.

Calum nearly burned his burger watching their antics rather than attending to his cooking.

Emmie exchanged an acknowledging nod with Calum, and she could see his green eyes spark as he gazed over at her. He wore a black, tight–fitting boxer's vest, black training trousers and dark trainers. He looked every inch a fighting fit champion. She liked Calum, but would her feelings for him ever be more than that?

Hunter hadn't yet noticed Calum, and she was assured that his playfulness wasn't a performance for Calum's benefit. But seeing her attention distracted, he followed her line of vision and saw

Calum. The two men exchanged a curt nod, then Hunter smiled, giving Emmie his full attention.

'Are you hungry?' Hunter said to her. 'Do you want to get something to eat before we make complete fools of ourselves in the contests?'

'How about a compromise,' she suggested. 'A light snack, then embarrass ourselves. Later we can enjoy the barbecue food while the winners polish their trophies.'

'Sounds like a plan.'

Taking her by surprise, Hunter clasped her hand and led her over to the nearest grill. Her senses reacted to the touch of his strong, elegant hands. An author's hands. Fingers that tapped at the keys of his laptop, creating stories for his books. She felt safe and assured when his long fingers wrapped around hers, claiming her, leading her, tempting her...

'What takes your fancy?' Hunter's words broke into her thoughts.

She blinked. Him, Hunter himself...

'Everything smells delicious,' he said. 'It's probably all the sea air.'

A sea breeze would've been handy, she thought, to cool her senses, but there was barely any. The night was a hot one, in more ways than one.

Hunter was looking at her. She jolted, hoping she hadn't said anything she was thinking.

She smiled and opted for a baked potato filled with cheese and coleslaw.

Hunter selected a chicken burger stacked with salad, red peppers and spicy sauce. And two teas.

Hunter donated generously to the fund. A request to give whatever you wanted towards the cost of the barbecue event. Then he led Emmie over to a couple of vacant chairs where they sat enjoying their food with a view of the sea and the activity buzzing along the shore.

'I've started reading your book, the first one in the series,' she told him. 'I became so engrossed in it that I couldn't put it down. When I realised the time, that you'd be coming to pick me up, I barely had time to throw my clothes off and run around the cottage to get ready.'

Hunter almost choked on his burger.

'Not that I usually run around stark naked,' she elaborated. 'What I mean is, to jump in the shower with no clothes on.' She started to feel flustered, and the more she tried to calm down, the bigger the pickle she got herself into.

Hunter could've intervened, saving her from embarrassing herself further, but he didn't. Shame on him.

'Of course I don't wear anything in the shower.'

Hunter couldn't drink his tea for snickering.

'But I don't want to talk about running around naked,' she insisted loudly.

'I should think not,' Ethel chided her. She glared at Hunter as if it was his fault that Emmie sounded irate.

Hunter went to object, but Ethel brushed any excuses aside as she told them, 'The three–legged race is about to kick off in a few minutes, so get your legs tied together. The competition is stiff this year.'

'Not as stiff as my joints,' the postmaster said, joining them. 'It's my own fault for sparring last night with Calum. But I went the distance with him.'

Ethel looked astounded. 'You were boxing Calum last night?'

'The boxing gloves you gave me fitted great,' the postmaster told Ethel.

Ethel shook her head at him. 'Silly old sausage. Why were you fighting Calum?'

'He challenged me. I couldn't sprout chicken feathers.'

'Though you do have chicken legs.' Calum's voice broke into the conversation.

Ethel nodded. 'But he has other impressive assets that more than make up for it.'

Emmie guffawed.

Ethel tried not to laugh. 'I was talking about his smile, and he's got nice hands for a man.'

Emmie gave her a look of — *yeah, right.*

An announcement that the race was due to commence soon saved them from further embarrassment.

'Are you running in the three–legged race?' the postmaster asked Calum.

'I'm hoping to,' Calum told him.

'Are you partnered with someone?' the postmaster added.

'Not yet, but I've got my eye on that fit wee blonde over there.' He pointed towards the woman of his choice.

Emmie and Ethel did a double take.

'Judith's a blonde!' Emmie exclaimed. 'When did that happen? I left the dressmaker's cottage in the middle of the afternoon, and she wasn't a blonde then.'

Ione overheard them as she walked past with her husband, Big Sam. 'I gave Judith and the dressmaker a wee boost of golden blonde colour after you left. Judith phoned me to say they were thinking of having me colour their hair again, so I popped over in the late afternoon. It didn't take long.'

'They both looked great the last time you coloured their hair,' said Ethel.

Ione nodded. 'Remember, don't let Judith get her hair wet in the sea. With her hair just coloured, it needs time to settle before she can go for a dip.'

'I'll remind her,' Emmie assured Ione.

'Are you two competing against us?' Big Sam asked Emmie and Hunter.

'We're going to give it a go,' Emmie confirmed.

Big Sam eyed up the competition and tightened the buckles on his kilt. Hunter was a fit looking man, but he felt confident that Ione and him could take them on.

As Ione and Big Sam headed away to get ready for the race, Calum ran over to Judith. She was talking to Hilda and Hilda's sister, Jessie, who was over from one of the nearby islands to attend the barbecue.

'Do you fancy tying yourself to me, Judith, and racing along the sand?' Calum asked her, running up to her.

'There's an offer, eh, Judith?' said Hilda.

Judith glanced round to see Calum standing there. 'I'm not a runner.'

'You can run fine,' Hilda told her.

Hilda then introduced her sister to Calum. 'This is my big sister, Jessie.'

Calum smiled. 'Cartwheels across the sand Jessie?' he queried.

The women laughed. He'd remembered what Hilda had said about her sister.

'So, how about it, Judith?' Calum dangled the ties for their ankles enticingly.

Judith pressed her lips together. 'I'll only slow you down.'

'Nonsense,' he said to her. As she continued to hesitate he added, 'Can you dance?'

'Dance? Eh, yes, but—'

'Waltz with me.' Without further hesitation, he took Judith in hold and began to waltz with her on the sand. 'See, you've got the rhythm. Now all you have to do is keep that sense of rhythm, keep in time with me when I'm running. Just go for it, Judith.'

'Okay, I'll give it my best,' she agreed.

'We might as well be contenders for the title while we're at it,' Calum said as he tied their ankles together.

'I can see why you're a competitive boxer.'

'Harangue me later, Judith. Let's give a good account of ourselves.'

As competitors began to line up for the start of the race, Emmie looked over at Calum. 'Why was Calum waltzing with Judith?' she said to Hunter.

Hunter shrugged. 'I've no idea.'

The postmaster shouted over to Emmie and Hunter. 'Come on you two.' He was already tied to Ethel.

'I'm nervous,' Emmie confessed as Hunter tied their ankles secure. They wrapped their arms around each other's waists. She felt the lean muscles under his shirt, and she wasn't sure whether the increased beating of her heart was due to the trepidation of the race, or being so close to Hunter.

'Don't be nervous, Emmie,' he assured her. 'You don't ever need to be nervous when you're with me.'

For some reason, his words calmed her, and she became alert, looking at the other couples on either side of them. They were sandwiched between Ione and Big Sam and Ethel and the postmaster. Next to the postmaster was Calum and Judith.

Aurora was nearby filming all the action. Bea was there with her boyfriend, Lewis, and a few of the sewing bee ladies were there with their men. Laughter and giggling filtered along the line as they waited for the starter's flag and whistle.

90

Hunter gave Emmie's waist an extra reassuring squeeze. Then for a second, he locked eyes with Calum. They exchanged a challenging glance, unseen by anyone else.

'Ready, steady...go!' the starter shouted through his megaphone and dropped his flag.

And they were off. Thundering towards the finishing line. Some stumbled and floundered. Others laughed all the way.

Big Sam and Ione couldn't keep up with Calum and Judith. Big Sam thought he had the race in the bag, but he could tell that they weren't going to win tonight.

Ethel and the postmaster gave a good performance, and were edging in front of Emmie and Hunter.

Emmie hadn't exaggerated when she said she was rubbish at the three–legged race. She could feel that her lack of ability was holding Hunter back, but she sensed he didn't mind. He'd wanted to beat Calum, but Calum was a fast runner and the competitive streak in him drove him on, taking Judith along for the ride.

People were cheering them on as they neared the finishing line. Many had tumbled and fallen by the wayside, others were lagging so far behind they were barely in the race, finishing only for the fun of it.

Aurora stood with her phone, filming the action, and the smile on Judith's face made her smile too.

As Calum and Judith crossed the line, clear winners, the crowd erupted in cheers. The boxing champ and Judith's names would be listed in the local village's recreation log as the winners that summer.

Calum could barely untie their legs because Judith was jumping up and down with excitement. 'I've never won a race in my puff!' she yelled gleefully.

In second place was Ethel and the postmaster, with Ione and Big Sam third.

Emmie wasn't sure whether they were fifth or not, but it didn't matter. They were never going to win.

Hunter untied them, but he seemed happy. So happy that he lifted Emmie up and swung her around, before putting her down and apologising. 'Sorry, I'm pumped up. That was fun.'

Emmie nodded. It was fun. Real fun, being with Hunter and with her new friends. The sense of community and the enjoyment they had from having a summer barbecue down the shore was wonderful.

In the spur of the moment, Hunter leaned down and kissed Emmie. She felt the passion ignite when his firm lips claimed hers.

Both of them blinked out of the moment and smiled at each other. Where did they go from here she wondered. What lay in store later that night? If an impromptu kiss sent her sensing reeling, what would her reaction be if they took things to the next level?

'Would the competitors now take their places for the egg and spoon race,' the starter announced.

'Are you up for it?' Hunter asked her.

Emmie shook her head. 'Nope.'

Hunter smiled. 'Lets go and get our eggs and spoons then.'

Smiling, she walked with Hunter to collect what they needed for the next race.

Judith was still bouncing with excitement and clutched the small trophy she'd been presented with by the postmaster.

'I'm going to get my name etched on it,' she said to Emmie, showing her the little gold winner's cup. 'I'll put it in my display cabinet in my living room.'

'I'm sure it'll look a treat,' said Emmie, feeling pleased for her.

'I can't wait to tell the dressmaker,' Judith enthused. 'But she's a busy bee tonight, working in her sewing room, finishing several dress designs. She's a fast worker, but I don't want to call and put her off her patterns.'

'You can tell her in the morning,' Emmie suggested.

Judith nodded firmly. 'Yes, I'll tell her while the kettle boils for our morning cuppa.' Still clutching her prize, she hurried away to show it to Ethel, Hilda and Ione.

'Hold it up and smile, Judith,' Aurora called to her. 'I've got a lovely view of the shimmering sea behind you in the background. It'll make for a gorgeous photo for the magazine. I'll put it in with your turquoise, sea theme tea cosy pattern.'

Thinking this was a great idea, Judith posed with the trophy as Aurora snapped the picture.

Several of them were gathered around, chatting, getting ready for the next race, and enjoying the fun of the night.

Calum was congratulated along with Judith.

'I've been tempted to read your latest book,' Ione said to Hunter.

'I hope you enjoy it,' he said.

'Big Sam has read it,' Ione continued. 'He knows what happens, and all the thrilling bits, so he's told me not to read it before I go to bed in case it gives me the collywobbles. So I'll read it during the day.'

The conversation quickly swung round to Ione's fear of things that go bump in the night.

'When I put the bedroom wall light out,' she confided to them, 'I take a run and flying leap in the dark into my bed. I know it's silly, but I've got this fear of there being monsters under the bed. Monsters that will grab your feet if you dangle them over the edge of the bed.'

'I still don't like my feet dangling off the end of the bed or exposed,' said Emmie.

A few of them nodded in agreement, disliking this themselves.

Ione shivered. 'It's the thought of monsters under the bed that gives me the heebie–jeebies.' She snuggled close to Big Sam as she said this.

Calum smiled at Ione and spoke with calm assurance. 'There are no monsters under the bed. Everyone knows they're always hiding in the wardrobe.'

Ione's eyes widened and lit up with trepidation. 'Don't say that!' She swiped Calum playfully on the arm.

Calum laughed, and the others enjoyed the friendly chatter.

'Now I'm going to have to check the wardrobe at night before I go to my bed,' said Ione. 'Checking under the bed for monsters and checking the wardrobe...' She sighed wearily. 'You've put the willies up me. I'm going to be bouncing around the bedroom for an hour before I get any sleep.'

'I thought that's what you did anyway,' Ethel joked with her, glancing between Ione and Big Sam.

Ione giggled and scolded her playfully. 'Ethel!'

'Grab your spoons, folks. The race is about to begin,' the starter announced.

Rushing to grab their eggs and spoons, they hurried over to compete. Almost everyone was taking part.

Except Judith. 'I'm quitting while I'm ahead. Going out on a win.' She held her trophy happily.

Leaving Judith to cheer them on from the sidelines, the others got ready to compete.

Ethel and the postmaster were poised for the race to the left of Emmie and Hunter, while Hilda, Jessie and Bea were lined up to her right. Others were standing nearby. Calum had opted out of the egg and spoon to man his grill and was busy cooking more burgers.

With seconds to go before the off, Emmie compared her egg and spoon to the ones Hunter had. 'I've got a smaller spoon and a larger egg than you.'

Before Hunter could offer to exchange these with her, Ethel commented. 'The postmaster has a big one too.'

'Thank you, Ethel,' the postmaster said, laughing.

Ethel gave him a scolding glance. But before any further discussion, the starter whistle blew.

Everyone got off to an equal start, but soon eggs were wobbling, toppling on the sand, and only those that managed to keep their eggs in their spoons were in the running. In the joint lead were Hunter and Big Sam, closely followed by a couple of the farmers.

Hunter narrowly held on to his lead and won the race.

Emmie ambled the last few steps, smiling in defeat, having lost her egg somewhere in the melée. She didn't mind and walked up to Hunter and gave him a congratulatory kiss on the cheek.

The moment was captured on camera by Aurora.

Hunter received an egg and spoon trophy, and a bonus gift — a set of egg cosies knitted and donated by Judith.

CHAPTER NINE

Barbecue Party

Hunter didn't embarrass himself in the sack.

Pitted against Calum, the postmaster, Big Sam, Lewis, and numerous men, including some of the fishermen and farmers, he gave a strong account of himself.

It was a pity he tried to wave to Emmie as she cheered him on, and lost his grip on his sack. Fumbling around in front of everyone, he then forced himself to forge ahead and finished in joint third place with Lewis. No shame with this, he thought.

Aurora's husband, Bredon the beemaster, was second. The cheers denoted he was a popular runner–up.

The race organisers hadn't been able to find a sack large enough to accommodate Big Sam, so when he galloped along the sand he had to grip his sack that hung around his thighs. This caused him to flounder and he tumbled over before reaching the finishing line.

'Your legs look like they been exfoliated,' Ione remarked to Big Sam as he stepped out of his sack.

He rubbed them down with his palms. 'The canvas sack was scratchy. I should've worn my troos and not my kilt.'

'I'll lather them with soothing lotion when we get home,' Ione promised him.

The crowd then cheered the winner as he went up to receive his trophy.

The men's sack race winner was Calum. His fitness, fighting tenacity and a stealthy method of handling his sack while he was running, led to his success.

Calum searched the faces in the cheering crowd for Emmie. And there she was, smiling up at Hunter, deep in conversation. Feeling as if his heart had a dagger through it, he waved and kept his smile firm. Then he went back to his grill, tucked the trophy in his sports bag, and continued to cook the barbecue food. He didn't take part in any of the other contests, preferring to get on with the cooking, and watching the fun unfold around him. Sometimes he caught a glimpse of Emmie and Hunter, both of them seemingly happy and engrossed in each other's company.

As the evening wore on, the scent of the barbecue food wafted along the shore, mixing with the sea air, churned up by a hint of a breeze drifting in from across the distant islands. Calum committed it all to memory, because soon that's all it would be. The fight was looming closer, and he'd have to start thinking of leaving.

'Your name has been pulled out the hat to front one of the men's tug of war teams, Calum,' the postmaster shouted over to him.

Two teams were lining up, all picked at random to keep the contest fair.

By chance, Hunter's name was selected to front the opposing team.

Calum and Hunter nodded to each other as they picked up the rope, grabbing it at the markers, as their teams lined up and grabbed hold of the rope behind them.

Behind Calum was the postmaster, Tavion the flower grower, recently back from a business trip away with Tiree, farmers, and their anchor was the tall, dark haired and handsome Cuan McVey the master chocolatier who'd supplied cakes and truffles for the barbecue.

Hunter was backed by Bredon the beemaster, Lewis, Fintry the flower hunter, fishermen and farmers, and their anchor was Big Sam the silversmith.

Everyone gathered to watch the final contest of the evening.

Emmie stood beside Bea, Mairead and Ione. Mairead nodded encouragement to Fintry, while Bea and Ione waved to Lewis and Big Sam. Aurora filmed them getting ready, including her husband, Bredon.

Hunter was talking over his shoulder to his team mates. Emmie watched them. Whatever Hunter was saying to them they nodded in agreement. She guessed they had a plan of action, and wondered if they would win. It was a strong team.

Equally strong was Calum's team. Ethel stood with Tiree and Mhairi. The postmaster was offering advice on how to grip the rope, and Cuan smiled over at his fiancée Mhairi as he anchored himself at the end of the line–up.

'We managed to get home in time for the barbecue,' Tiree told Ethel.

'Did Tavion's business trip to Edinburgh go well?' Ethel asked her.

'It did,' said Tiree. 'I never realised there was so much work at this time of year for Tavion's flower growing, but hopefully now that his deals are settled, I'll have more time to help the dressmaker.'

'Emmie's been helping her,' Ethel assured her.

'I know, but I'm the dressmaker's apprentice. I feel I've let her down,' Tiree confided.

'She doesn't think that. Judith told me that the dressmaker wants you to focus on your romance with Tavion,' said Ethel.

'Well, I'm home now, so I'll help more with the dresses for the television series. I've heard they're beautiful designs.'

'I haven't seen them, but Judith and Emmie say the designs are gorgeous,' Ethel explained.

'I'll pop up to the cottage soon and help when I can,' Tiree promised.

'Get set,' the starter announced.

Hunter and Calum faced each other as their teams prepared for the challenge of strength and sheer determination to pull their opponents over the winning marker.

'Take the strain,' the starter shouted. 'Ready...' The crowd held their breath. 'Pull!'

The tug of war began.

At first, they seemed evenly matched, neither team moving the other any great distance.

Calum's green eyes stared directly at the ice blue daggers Hunter was glaring at him. Aware of Emmie standing there watching them, there was more at stake for them than just winning the contest.

The fierce competitive spirit in Calum ignited as he heard Emmie's voice cheer them on. Was she cheering for Hunter? Or him? He knew the answer, and this made him all the more determined not to be beaten by Hunter's team.

'Anchor! Hold the line!' Calum roared, urging Cuan McVey to dig his heels hard into the sand, and lean back with the rope wrapped around his waist. The chocolatier dug in, anchoring his team, giving them the leverage they needed to pull the rope in their direction.

Challenging them, Hunter countered by roaring encouragement to his team. 'Come on, gentlemen. Pull! Pull!'

Both teams gave it everything they had, resulting in an exhausting standoff, where one side gained the advantage, pulling their opponents off their mark. Then the challengers fought back hard and pulled their opponents off kilter.

The postmaster had taken part in these tug of wars since he was a young man, but in all his years of experience, he'd never seen two teams so well matched, and equally determined not to give an inch.

Fintry the flower hunter, fit to the core from his years sailing around the world in search of rare flowers and plants, backed up the equally strong Lewis and Bredon the Beemaster. The three tall, blond haired figures pulled together, sandwiched between their kilted anchor, Big Sam, and front man, Hunter. The voices of their wives and girlfriends rang loud amid the cheering — Mairead, Bea, Ione and Aurora.

'Come on, Fintry!' Mairead shouted.

Aurora wanted to shout to Bredon, but didn't because her camera would wobble.

Bea yelled encouragement to Lewis, while Ione wished that Big Sam hadn't gone commando. The pleats in his kilt were swinging higher and higher as he leaned back to anchor the team.

'One minute!' shouted the starter, checking the time.

'What does that mean?' Emmie asked Ione.

'There's a time limit,' Ione explained. 'If neither team can win within that time, they call it a draw.'

Both teams put in extra effort, resulting in an even surer standoff, with neither team gaining a clear win.

The crowd cheered until the final whistle blew, signalling the tug of war was over.

'A draw!' the starter declared.

The roar of the crowd showed they were happy with the decision. Both teams put on a great performance, and it seemed fitting that they shared the triumph.

As they let go of the rope and shook hands with each other, Big Sam was still anchored to it. When they let go he tumbled back on to the sand and the front of his kilt flew up.

He quickly covered his particulars and stood up. 'Sorry folks. I didn't mean to flash my periwinkle.'

The laughter and applause erupted.

With the contests finished, the night continued with the barbecues being fired up and music started playing for the dancing.

Hunter walked over to Emmie after thanking his team for their efforts. All contestants in the tug of war were presented with winner rosettes.

Emmie smiled at Hunter and insisted he pin his rosette to his shirt. 'You were amazing.' She helped him pin it on his shirt.

Hunter gazed down at her. 'Amazing, huh?'

'Well, you were okay, sort of, I suppose,' she joked with him.

He clasped his hand over hers as she finished pinning the rosette and pressed it against his heart.

She felt his strength beneath her hand. 'Your heart is thundering.'

He looked at her with those incredible blue eyes. 'Not from the tug of war.'

He was about to kiss her when his phone rang. 'I'll let it ring.'

'Take it. Maybe it's important.'

He checked the caller and sighed. 'It's my agent. Would you mind if I take this?'

'Not at all,' she assured him. 'I'll get you a cold drink. You'll need it after all that effort.'

She walked away to give him a few minutes of privacy to take the call.

'Two iced lemonades, please,' she said to one of the stallholders serving refreshments.

'I'll have one of those as well,' Calum said over her shoulder.

She looked round to see him gazing at her, unsure what to do, what to say...

'I'm glad the tug of war was a draw,' she told him, filling in the awkward gap.

'Two great teams,' he acknowledged.

'They were. Maybe you'll win next year?' Her voice was tense, sensing that he cared for her, but knowing she'd become involved with Hunter.

'I don't think I'll be here next year.' The heaviness in his tone was evident.

'No, you'll be off fighting for more championship titles all over the world.' She tried to sound chirpy, while feeling the opposite.

'We'll see,' he said.

She didn't know what else to say, and her heart ached for all the reasons she couldn't quite understand. She was falling for Hunter, and yet...if she'd met Calum first without Hunter on the scene, would her future have been with this handsome fighter?

Calum picked up his glass of lemonade and proposed a toast. The only proposal he'd make to Emmie...sweet, sexy, beautiful Emmie. 'To what might have been.'

He tipped his glass against hers before she had a chance not to accept such a toast. It seemed so final, so sad.

By now Hunter had finished his call and came striding over to join them. He accepted one of the glasses of lemonade that Emmie was holding. He took a long drink of it, put his arm around Emmie's shoulder and smiled pleasantly to Calum. 'I think you made Judith's night winning the three–legged race. She's still bouncing.'

Calum smiled. 'She ran well.'

'She suits being a blonde,' Emmie remarked.

'She does,' Calum agreed.

The tension felt awkward, so Hunter indicated towards two yachts in the harbour nearby. 'Fintry and Lewis are helping raise funds for the barbecue. They're offering to take couples sailing along the shore. Want to go?' he asked Emmie.

Calum smiled and faded into Emmie's past as he walked away to join the postmaster, Ethel, Judith and others. He didn't look back. He didn't want to see Emmie wrapped up in Hunter. The blood was roaring through his veins, in despair, in acceptance. He had to put all his energies now into his forthcoming fight. His contest with Hunter was over. Hunter won.

As Hunter and Emmie walked along the shore towards the yachts in the harbour, he told her about his phone call.

'My agent wants me to fly to London for talks with the film company.'

'The one that's interested in making your books into a film?'

'Yes. He sounds hopeful that we'll secure a movie deal with franchise potential.'

'For further films based on your spy thriller series of books?'

He nodded. 'It's what we've been planning for. The conference calls went well, as I said to you, but now they want to sit down and chat with me face to face.'

'When do you leave?' She was happy for him, but expected it wasn't an urgent meeting.

'Tomorrow. My agent has arranged for me to have dinner with the producers and directors tomorrow night in London.'

'So soon?' She tried and failed to hide the disappointment in her voice.

'I'm sorry.' He didn't pretend that it wasn't bad timing. To leave when they were just getting to know each other. But he intended coming back, sometime, though his schedule was flexible. He hadn't told her yet, but they'd mentioned he'd probably have to fly to New York for further talks if the meeting in London went well with their investors.

It felt like the sound of the sea was rushing through her, washing over her, drowning her in waves of suppressed tears, sadness and resentment at her own stupidity. When would she ever learn? Every time she met someone and thought that romantic happiness was within her grasp, a tidal wave of reality swept it away, leaving her wrung out and on her own yet again. Fool her for trusting Hunter. Shame on him for knowing there was a good chance he'd be leaving for London, but was prepared to make her believe they could have a loving relationship.

'Emmie, I'm sorry. We can still be—'

She cut–in. 'I'm sorry too. I can't do this, Hunter. I just can't go down that road again. Not now. I came here to feel better about things. And yes, I am stubborn, but I think I have ample reason to be as I am. And so...' she stepped back from him. 'I wish you all the success in the world. But I just can't risk falling in love for nothing.'

She walked away, hugging her arms around herself, trying to contain the shivers, the shock. One minute she'd felt all the happiness of the evening, and then had it shattered. Same old story. Hunter should write a better ending. She doubted he ever would.

Hunter remained where he was. Silent. He didn't call her name, or try to wangle his way out of the situation he'd caused. She was right. He'd known there was a strong chance that his agent was about to secure a film deal with the production company and that a meeting in London was on the cards. He should've told her, warned her, assured her that it was okay. He'd go there and come back, to finish his novel, to continue where they'd left off. He should have, but he didn't. And he knew the reason why. Emmie's reaction. He feared if he told her, she wouldn't want to date him. He didn't blame her for walking away. The blame was his.

Emmie walked through the hub of the barbecue. The aroma of the cooking filled the air, but she couldn't detect it. She heard the chatter and laughter of the people, but she didn't know a word of what they were saying.

She kept on walking, far along the shore, feeling calmer the further she went, until she dared to stop and look back at how far she'd come. The chatter was drowned out by the gentle sound of the sea. The lights of the barbecue glowed in the distance, and the sound of the music as people were dancing filtered along the coast, barely audible by the time it reached her.

She sat down on the sand, tired, drained. And wept. Silly of her, she thought. Wiping away the tears, she sat there on her own gazing out at the sea, trying to settle, to regain her strength.

That night, the dressmaker was busy in her sewing room, working on the dresses. She'd always loved sewing in the evenings, cosy in her cottage, tucked away within the forest. The lamps gave a glow to the fabric, emphasising the beautiful colours, and she sat at one of the sewing machines, stitching fast and accurate thin hems along the edges of a chiffon evening dress.

The sound of the machine had a tendency to lull Thimble to sleep, and he was snuggled up asleep nearby.

The dressmaker had almost finished a classic tea dress. The darts in the bodice were done, sleeves inserted, pretty collar attached, and it only needed the hems and sash finished. She'd ask Emmie to finish those in the morning.

Her latest sketch book lay open on the table next to her sewing machine. She'd been inking new designs with such finesse that they looked like fashion illustrations fit for printing as artwork.

She worked with the windows open, and the scent of the forest wafted in on the warm night air. There was barely a breeze, and she wore a cool cotton shift dress. Her newly blonded hair shone under the lights, a shimmering blonde, a fair match for her natural colour without the silver. Each time she caught a glimpse of herself in the mirror, she was taken aback by her appearance. Always elegant, it was nice to be a bit more glamorous if only for the summer.

She checked the time. The night was wearing on. She hoped the barbecue party was going well. She imagined Emmie, Ethel and some of the other sewing bee ladies would be surprised to see that Judith was a blonde. She smiled to herself, imagining the stories Judith would have to tell her in the morning.

It was disconcerting when a breeze blew in the window, causing her to pause from sewing. Whatever it was disturbed Thimble and he was now awake and alert.

The dressmaker went over and closed the window, gazing out into the depths of the forest. And she sensed...something was wrong.

The scent of the forest greenery lingered in the sewing room. The dressmaker sighed heavily, picked up her phone and went to call Judith. She hesitated, not wanting to spoil everyone's fun night down the shore. And yet...

Sighing again, she put her phone away and went through to the kitchen to make a cup of tea. She wasn't always right about the things she sensed.

While the kettle boiled she went through to the living, opened the patio doors and breathed in the beautiful summer night.

Thimble padded out into the garden, as he often did, jumped over the hedge and disappeared into the greenery.

The dressmaker closed the patio doors, made herself a cup of tea, cut a slice of Dundee cake and ate it in the kitchen before going back through to the sewing room to work.

One of the lamps flickered and dimmed for a moment. She paused, glanced around, shrugged off whatever she was sensing, and continued with her sewing.

CHAPTER TEN

The Dressmaker's Cottage

'Ginger wine?' Calum exclaimed, holding up his glass having taken a drink. 'This is potent stuff, Ethel. What's in it? Whisky?'

Ethel tightened her shawl around her shoulders. 'There's a wee splash of whisky in it.'

'And cognac, rum and probably brandy,' Judith added. 'Ethel's ginger wine has more than just raspberry essence in it.'

Some of the sewing bee ladies were gathered, chatting and enjoying a drink at the barbecue with Calum and the postmaster.

Calum had stopped looking for Emmie and Hunter, having had his heart fried enough for one evening. Besides, he hadn't seen either of them for a while now, and surmised they'd be strolling hand in hand along the shore, or whatever else they were up to.

While they were laughing and enjoying themselves, Fintry the flower hunter came striding up to them from the harbour. Lewis was with him. The serious expressions on their faces brought the chatter to a halt.

'Hilda,' Fintry began, 'I think you should warn your sister, Jessie, not to sail home tonight to the island with her husband.'

'What's wrong?' Hilda asked him, sounding concerned. Jessie and her husband were dancing to lively ceilidh music with other couples nearby.

'A storm's coming,' said Fintry. 'I've decided not to take my boat out tonight. Folk will be disappointed, but I fear it's not safe.' He glanced at Lewis. 'We're keeping our boats in the harbour. We'll sail another night.'

Lewis nodded. 'Fintry has more experience than me when it comes to sailing in wild seas, and he knows this coast better than me.' He shivered. 'But there's something in the atmosphere that feels like a storm is brewing.'

Fintry pointed to the islands far out in the sea and the sweeping coastline. At first glance it looked like a lovely calm night, with the twilight sun glinting off the water.

The postmaster looked at the view. 'It seems like a wonderful, warm night to me.'

'It is,' Fintry agreed. 'But look at those clouds way out over the islands, and the darkening sky on the far horizon. See the thunder clouds rolling in fast?'

Everyone looked to see what Fintry was meaning.

The postmaster's eyebrows raised and he stared at the fast–moving storm clouds. 'This is moving in fast.'

'Too fast,' Lewis added. 'If we'd taken the yachts out, we'd be lucky to make it back to the harbour before the storm hits the coast.'

Hilda sounded flustered. 'I'll warn Jessie and her man. They can stay the night with me at my house.' She ran off to tell them.

'What can I do to help?' asked Calum.

'Help spread the word, without causing panic,' said Fintry. 'Folk understand what the storms here can be like. Find Tavion, ask him to tell the farmers. Lewis and I will warn the fishermen to secure their boats in the harbour. And ask Big Sam and Cuan McVey to organise clearing the barbecue equipment. Get everything and everyone off the sand, away from the shore. Don't hang around the esplanade. The water will wash right over it if the storm is as bad as I think it will be.'

Calum nodded and didn't hesitate. He hurried to find Tavion and Cuan, and warn the others.

'You're welcome to come over to my cottage to shelter,' Ethel said to the sewing bee ladies and the postmaster. Most of them had walked down to the shore, leaving their cars at home, thinking they'd meander back up after the barbecue, so they were happy to take Ethel up on her offer.

Hunter approached, wondering what was happening. Fintry told him.

Hunter frowned and glanced around. 'Where's Emmie?'

'We thought she was with you,' said the postmaster.

'The two of you were kissing and engrossed in each other the last I saw,' Ethel added.

The guilt cut across Hunter's handsome features. 'We had a falling out. I upset her and she went for a walk along the shore to be on her own.'

Fintry scanned the coastline. 'What way did she go?'

Hunter pointed. 'Along there.'

105

Fintry bit his lip. 'Is she a strong swimmer?'

No one knew.

'Can she swim?' Fintry added.

No one knew that either.

'She wasn't going for a swim,' Hunter insisted. 'She just wanted to calm down and be on her own.'

'She may not have a choice. There's a cove down there and she could become cut off by the sea on both sides. The currents are strong.'

Hunter's heart turned to ice.

'You shouldn't have let her wander off on her own,' the postmaster chided Hunter.

Hunter didn't argue. The postmaster was right. He cursed himself for his own stupidity. He phoned her, but there was no reply. He shook his head.

'She could've gone back to her cottage,' Ethel suggested.

'I'm going to batten the hatches on the post office. I'll see if she's there,' the postmaster told Hunter.

Hunter nodded. 'I'll go and look for her along the shore.'

'I'll go with you,' said Bredon. He'd heard what was happening. 'And can you take Aurora with you, Ethel?' He motioned nearby. Aurora was taking pictures of the approaching storm for the magazine. 'Nail her down. You know what she's like. We don't want a repeat of the last time.'

Ethel and the others knew that Aurora had a reputation for being a troublemaker. During a previous storm, she'd almost been swept off the esplanade when trying to film the waves washing up over the sea wall.

'I'll make sure,' Ethel told Bredon. She called over to her. 'Aurora, come on with us.'

Hunter's heart felt chilled as he hurried away with Bredon to search the coastline for Emmie.

Big Sam and Cuan McVey came running over to Ethel and the others. Big Sam had a tight grip on Ione.

'Would you take Ione with you, Ethel?' Big Sam handed Ione to Ethel's safe keeping.

Ione was trying not to show how nervous she was. 'I don't mind storms, the wind, the rain. But thunder storms terrify me.'

As if on cue, the low rumble of thunder was heard in the distance, followed by the first flash of lightning across the sea. The air sounded as if it had been split with a thunderbolt.

Ione gasped.

Ethel pulled her close. 'You'll be safe with us. It's just a wee storm. Come on, we're going over to my cottage.'

Cuan McVey's cottage was near Ethel's cottage and he'd made it available too. Mhairi was taking people over to the chocolatier's cottage while Cuan helped clear the shore.

Judith tried phoning Emmie, but there was no reply. She watched Hunter and Bredon head away along the shore in search of her.

Hunter hurried along the sand, scanning the coastline. 'Emmie!' He shouted her name repeatedly. The rising wind blew his voice out to sea.

'I don't see any sign of her,' said Bredon. 'I doubt she walked further along the coast at night. She's probably at her cottage. We should head back.'

Hunter nodded reluctantly, and they walked briskly back to join the others.

The postmaster came back from putting up the storm shutters on the windows of the post office. 'Emmie's not in her cottage,' he told Hunter.

Hunter couldn't think where she could be.

'Does anyone have a car available?' a man called down to the shore from the esplanade.

'I do,' Hunter shouted to him. 'What do you need?' He started to walk up to the esplanade while Bredon helped Big Sam and Cuan clear the shore.

The man, one of the farmers, had his arms around the shoulders of two women, with a third woman standing beside them.

'Could you take my wife, my mother and my gran home? We're in one of the farmhouses. I didn't bring my car down. We didn't expect a storm.' They'd intended walking home after the barbecue, a leisurely walk after enjoying the night. But the storm changed everything, and now he wanted them home safely before the storm quickened.

'Yes, I'll be right there,' Hunter told him, running over to where he'd parked his car outside Emmie's cottage. He jumped in, spun the car around, and picked up the passengers. Driving them up to their farmhouse, he drove back down to the shore and offered to take others home quickly. A few accepted his offer of help, and he was kept busy for the next while. It also gave him a chance to scour the area looking for Emmie.

Judith stood at the front door of Ethel's cottage. The phone signal was becoming weaker, and standing outside helped her connect with the dressmaker. The call was short.

'Emmie's gone missing.' Judith told her the news.

The dressmaker sounded understandably upset. 'She doesn't know this area well enough to go wandering off.'

'She'd fallen out with Hunter.'

'Has anyone seen her?'

'No.' Judith paused, wondering why the dressmaker hadn't sensed that there would be a storm.

'I didn't want to spoil everyone's fun at the barbecue,' the dressmaker explained without being asked. 'And I wasn't entirely sure. I sensed a change in the atmosphere while I was sewing, but...' She shrugged, wishing she'd phoned Judith to warn her, to warn everyone.

'It's not your fault.' Judith knew the dressmaker would blame herself if anything happened to Emmie.

The dressmaker blamed herself anyway.

'The signal's starting to break up,' said Judith, watching the dark, thunderous clouds fold over the islands, darkening the sea and heading straight for the coast.

'Call me with any news,' the dressmaker managed to say before the signal cut out.

She sat down in her sewing room wondering what to do.

Emmie drove further into the forest, unaware of the storm or the trouble brewing. After walking along the shore, she'd decided to drive up to the dressmaker's cottage and help with the sewing. No doubt the dressmaker was working busily while everyone enjoyed the barbecue party. Feeling upset and unsettled, she figured she'd keep the dressmaker company and finish some of the sewing.

Her car headlights illuminated the narrow road through the forest. She was sure this was the right route, but then again, all the trees and greenery looked similar. The headlamps also had a

108

tendency to highlight the trees so much that they looked entirely different from during the day.

Now spits of rain were hitting off the front windshield, making it even more difficult to navigate and find a familiar route.

She thought she caught a glimpse of the dressmaker's cottage through the trees, but the road was too narrow to drive the car there. So rather than continue to drive in circles, she stopped and stepped out, determined to walk through the gap in the greenery to the cottage.

A breeze blew through the trees and the leaves fluttered in the wind. The rain became heavier, but the canopy of trees acted like an umbrella, shielding her from the worst of it.

As she continued on, she glanced around and realised she'd lost her way, and the further she walked, whether in circles or not, she couldn't find her way to the cottage or her way back to her car.

She hugged her arms around herself for futile comfort and warmth, and decided to shelter under one of the trees to gain her sense of direction. But the thick trees and greenery and shadowed darkness prevented her from finding her way safely back to her car, or the dressmaker's cottage.

She tried to phone for assistance, but there was no signal.

The rain started to increase, and the sounds of the storm began to rustle the leaves, and made her feel vulnerable.

Pressing her back against one of the trees, she took a deep breath and tried to think what to do. She felt in jeopardy, and she'd never been in a situation like this before.

She'd pictured everyone dancing and enjoying the barbecue party, but she assumed the storm was even stronger down on the shore without the trees to shield the worst of it.

And she thought about Hunter. Would he be looking for her? Would Calum?

Calum came striding across the sand to where Hunter and several other men, including Big Sam and Cuan were checking the shore for the last of the partygoers. No one was left. They'd all gone home or were sheltering in Ethel or Cuan's cottages.

'Where's Emmie?' Calum asked them.

'She's missing,' said Big Sam.

'Missing?' Calum glared daggers at Hunter. 'Wasn't she with you?'

Big Sam intervened, sensing that an argument could kick off.

'Hunter and Emmie had a wee tiff,' Big Sam explained. 'She went to cool her engine with a walk along the shore. No one has seen her since.'

Calum faced Hunter with a look of fury. 'If anything happens to her...'

'I didn't know there was a storm pending,' Hunter told Calum.

'You should've been looking after her,' Calum shouted at him. 'Storm or no storm, you shouldn't have let her wander along the shore at night on her own, especially as she's not familiar with this area.'

Hunter didn't argue. Calum was right, but that didn't change anything. Emmie was still missing.

'What way did she go?' asked Calum.

Hunter pointed in the direction she'd gone.

Without further hesitation, Calum ran off, fast and determined to find her, or at least try.

'We've already checked,' Hunter shouted after him. 'She's not there.'

Calum didn't stop, powering away along the shore, a strong and determined silhouette against the glimmering sea.

Hunter watched him, his intense blue eyes darkening with the storm raging inside him. He felt conflicted. He was sure Emmie wasn't there, and yet... He shook the doubts of his own decisions from his thoughts. There had to be a better way to find Emmie than running wild along the coast.

Calum reached the area where she'd stopped to sit down on the sand. There was no trace of her. With the panic in his heart burning through him he shouted against the fierce wind. 'Emmie! Emmie!'

The dressmaker couldn't settle in the sewing room. She jolted, sensing something far in the distance.

Wishing she'd phoned Judith to warn her of her feelings that there was an impending storm, she wandered through to the living room and gazed out the patio doors into the garden. The doors were locked against the increasing wind. She watched the rain hit off the windows and the flowers and trees blow wildly. She knew that if this was the strength of the storm in the heart of the forest, it was going to be fierce and wild down on the shore.

Thimble hadn't come back from his night–time prowl.

And then she saw him, running quickly across the garden towards the closed patio doors.

The dressmaker opened the doors a fraction to let him in without letting the howling wind in too.

But Thimble didn't want to come in. He meowed loudly, ran away across the garden to the edge of the forest, then repeated this process, running back to the patio doors.

The dressmaker got the message.

She hurried through to the cloakroom in the hallway and put on a long, waterproof hooded coat and a pair of sturdy boots. Unhooking a small pre–packed rucksack from a hook, she shrugged it up on her shoulder and then followed Thimble into the forest.

The lights shining from the windows and patio doors of the cottage illuminated the garden and the beams filtered further to where the garden merged with the lush greenery. But as she walked deeper into the forest the light was fading fast. The overhanging trees helped buffer the ferocity of the howling wind and provided an umbrella against the rain. Patches of the ground, gnarled with tree roots and moss were dry, while other areas were more exposed to the elements and were damp and glistening wet in the stormy twilight.

The dressmaker paused and dug out a sturdy torch from her bag, flicked it on and shone the beam all around her. Venturing into the dark forest on a stormy night was not for the faint–hearted, but with calm determination, and a strength few realised she still had from her earlier years, she continued to follow Thimble as he led the way into what she knew was a precarious part of the forest. A narrow stream ran through the undergrowth causing shallow puddles and an unsteady route to trudge on. But she knew the forest well, and she felt in her heart that someone needed her help. That instinct of hers was switched up to the hilt. There were times when she questioned her so–called gift, but not tonight. If her instincts were right, Emmie was here, and in trouble.

The torch beam hit off the trees, flashing through the darkness. The rain was becoming heavier. She could only imagine how fierce the storm was down on the shore. At least the forest offered some protection.

111

Thimble ran ahead quickly, then stopped and glanced back at the dressmaker. His green eyes shone in the beam of the torch. He meowed urgently.

'Emmie!' the dressmaker called out, trusting Thimble to lead the way.

Emmie blinked against the rain that was stinging her eyes. The wind blew through her hair and she swept it back to peer into the trees. Was she hearing things? It sounded like a woman had shouted her name.

'Emmie!'

There it was again, closer this time.

'I'm over here,' Emmie shouted back. She'd pressed her back against a sturdy tree and hugged her arms around herself for warmth. She could hear the rain batter off the leaves, but at least the greenery offered an umbrella that shielded her from the full force of the rainstorm.

She blinked against the rain that hit her face, and saw the beam of a torch shine in the distance. A glimpse, and then it was gone again.

'Help! I'm over here!' she repeated, hoping they would find her. She'd decided to wait out the storm where she was, the best shelter she could find, instead of wandering around the forest and endangering herself further. She shouldn't have left the safety of her car, but she'd been so sure that she'd seen the dressmaker's cottage nearby. But getting lost was so easy, and so frightening, especially when she heard the thunder and saw flashes of lighting tear across the sky. Standing under a tree wasn't her ideal choice, but it seemed better than getting totally soaked and risking falling down a gulley.

The torch shone bright and Emmie shielded her eyes against the beam of light, peering to see the person holding it.

The dressmaker? Was she seeing things? And she was on her own. Well, Thimble was with her.

The cat ran over to Emmie. He'd found his target and sat loyally at her feet, a marker for the dressmaker to find her.

And she did. The dressmaker smiled with relief, but was aware that Emmie was soaked and shivering, and no doubt suffering from mild shock from the situation.

'Emmie, are you hurt?'

'No, I was driving up to the cottage, but I got lost. I shouldn't have left my car—'

'Where is your car?'

Emmie shrugged and glanced around her. 'I don't know. I'm totally lost. I'm not sure what way I came. The trees all look the same, and then it became darker, and the rain was heavier, and I sort of panicked—'

'Come with me. The cottage isn't too far away.' She shrugged her rucksack off, opened it and pulled out a folded raincoat, a thin fabric, but sufficient for providing enough coverage against the rain. 'Put this on.'

Emmie didn't hesitate. She put it on, zipped it tight and pulled up the hood. It was large enough to have accommodated a man like Hunter, but she welcomed wearing it.

With Thimble again leading the way, the dressmaker and Emmie forged their way back to the cottage. The dressmaker knew the route, but used Thimble as a compass to quicken their journey.

The lights of the cottage shone through the greenery, and Emmie, now linking arms with the dressmaker, smiled with relief at the welcoming glow.

'We're nearly there, Emmie.'

The dressmaker had encouraged her every step of the way. The wind battered against them as they had to venture across areas where the trees were sparse and this exposed them to the full force of the wind and rain.

Hurrying on, the dressmaker opened the patio doors and the three of them went inside. She closed the doors firmly and locked them.

In the hallway they took off their wet coats, boots and shoes. The dressmaker's outfit had kept her dry, but Emmie was soaked, as was Thimble.

'Jump in the shower,' the dressmaker told Emmie, ushering her through to one of the spare bedrooms that had an en suite bathroom. She flicked the lamps on in the bedroom. It had a quilted bedspread and quilted cushions on a chair beside the window. The room was beautifully clean and tidy.

'Throw your wet clothes in the wash basket. You'll find clean clothes in the wardrobes and drawers. Help yourself. Though I think it's best you stay the night until the storm subsides, so there are nightgowns and socks you can wear if you decide to stay.'

113

'Thank you. I'd appreciate staying here until the morning.'

Nodding for Emmie to hurry up and get out of her wet things, the dressmaker walked away, having grabbed a towel for Thimble.

Bedraggled, but otherwise alert and happy that he'd helped find Emmie, Thimble relished the attention lavished on him by the dressmaker. She wrapped him up in the fluffy towel and dried his fur, gave him something to eat and drink and then tucked him up in his little basket that was lined with a quilt the sewing bee ladies had made for him.

Emmie came padding through to the kitchen after showering. She wore a vintage style cotton nightgown and comfy socks. She'd towel dried her hair and brushed it through. Her face was scrubbed clean, and she looked even younger and prettier without any makeup.

The dressmaker had made a pot of strong tea and hot buttered toast. 'Help yourself to the toast,' she said while pouring their tea.

Emmie sat down at the kitchen table and helped herself to a slice of toast, and sipped her tea.

They sat in the cosy kitchen and chatted.

'I phoned Judith to tell her you're safe,' said the dressmaker. 'Judith will tell everyone you've been found. They thought you were missing down the shore and they've been looking for you.'

Emmie stared in surprise. 'People thought I'd gone missing?'

'Yes, Hunter took the brunt of the blame for letting you wander off along the coast on your own at night.'

'It wasn't his fault. I just wanted to be on my own. We'd fallen out. His agent phoned when we were enjoying the barbecue. Hunter has to leave tomorrow for meetings in London with a film company. They're interested in making his books into a movie.' She explained the details.

The dressmaker poured them more tea. 'Romance is never easy.'

The relief washed over Hunter, knowing that Emmie was safe. 'Thanks for telling me, Judith.'

'Are you still leaving tomorrow?' she said.

'I have to. It's what I've been working for — a film deal. But I'll be coming back.' He didn't specify when.

Hunter's vague attitude made Judith frown.

'I promise I will come back,' he insisted.

114

CHAPTER ELEVEN

Quilting and Embroidery

Hunter went back to his cottage. He was tempted to phone Emmie, but it was late at night and Judith had advised him to leave it until the morning. Not wanting to disturb Emmie or the dressmaker, he decided to get some sleep and talk to her in the morning before he left for London.

Emmie was tucked up in bed, under a patchwork quilt, in the dressmaker's cottage. Rain hit off the windows and the wind blew through the trees in the forest, but she felt safe and cosy. She thought about the events of the evening, and about Hunter. Her heart fluttered when she thought of him kissing her, catching her when she jumped over the sea wall, lifting her up and swinging her around smiling, happy. Until his agent called they'd been happy. She wondered if Hunter would call her before leaving for London.

Listening to the sound of the rain, she fell asleep and didn't wake up until the morning.

Fortunately, the storm hadn't caused any structural damage. The waves washing over the sea wall had brought with them seaweed, sand and driftwood, but this was cleaned up early in the morning by numerous members of the local community. They made short work of it.

Bunting was tied along the esplanade and once again the shore looked bright, breezy and welcoming.

Hunter had cycled down to assess the damage, and got roped into helping restring the bunting from the lamplights.

The air felt particularly fresh, as if the storm had cleared the residue of heat, and everything looked summery and clean. The scent of the flowers in Tavion's field, and the greenery from other fields nearby, created a heady fragrance. The flowers had welcomed the downpour in the heart of the hot summer. Now everything looked and smelled fresh.

Hunter hadn't slept well, dwelling on thoughts of Emmie and the mess he'd made of things. He hoped she'd want to talk to him before he left. Unsure of what would happen between them, he cycled back up to his cottage, packed his bags, loaded them into his car and drove up to see Emmie at the dressmaker's cottage.

Emmie had been up early, feeling a lot better about everything that had happened. She wore a lovely floral print dress that the dressmaker hung on her wardrobe door for her.

'This should fit you nicely, Emmie, while your clothes are in the wash.'

'Thank you so much...for everything.'

The dressmaker smiled. 'I've made breakfast. Judith should be here soon, but come and have something to eat.'

Emmie got dressed quickly and admired her reflection in the full–length mirror. The dress fitted her well, and she wore the fluffy socks with it. Brushing her hair, she added a touch of makeup, and then went through to the kitchen.

A fresh pot of tea was on the table and there was the homely aroma of toast being grilled.

'I'm having porridge,' the dressmaker told Emmie. There's cereal if you prefer—'

'No, I'd like porridge.'

The dressmaker shared the hot porridge between two bowls. 'There's creamy milk in the fridge and fresh brambles and strawberries. And heather honey if you want it.'

Emmie poured the creamy milk on her porridge and added the fresh fruit.

The toast was ready for buttering, and Emmie spread butter and heather honey of one of the thick slices.

Pouring the tea, the dressmaker sat down at the kitchen table and chatted about the day ahead.

'I worked on some of the dresses last night, but I've left the embroidery for you.'

'Great, I'll get on with it after breakfast,' said Emmie, eager to start work to take her mind off dwelling on Hunter. She didn't want to think that he was probably packing his bags and driving off right now. Would she ever see him again? Or was it over between them?

Over the rim of her teacup the dressmaker read the turmoil in Emmie. 'Whatever it's worth, make the decisions that suit you.'

Emmie nodded. 'I will.'

'And that includes me. Don't miss out on any chances you're offered because you feel you're letting me down.'

Emmie frowned. 'I've no intention of letting you down.'

'I invited you here because I wanted to give you something, as a thank you for contacting me and bringing my dresses here.'

Emmie wasn't sure what she meant.

Before they could continue, Judith came bustling in. 'How are you, Emmie? Are you feeling okay after being caught in the storm? It must've been quite traumatic getting lost in the forest at night, in the rain. Still, you're looking well and I see you're having a bowl of porridge. That'll set you up for the day. It's going to be another scorcher. The storms always clear the air.' She breathed deeply. 'Has Hunter phoned you yet? He was going to call last night, but I advised him to leave it until the morning.'

Emmie had her phone switched on and had checked for messages. 'No, he hasn't called or left a message.' She tried to hide the disappointment in her voice.

The dressmaker and Judith exchanged a glance, and Judith changed the subject. 'What are we working on this morning?' she said chirpily.

'Emmie's going to finish the embroidery while I work on the next couple of dresses.'

Judith smiled and rubbed her palms together. 'Great. I'm knitting the tippets, and I've buttons to sew on to one of the cardigans.' She was just about to pour a cup of tea when the doorbell rang.

The three women glanced at each other. It had to be Hunter.

'I'll see if it's him,' said Judith. 'Do you want to talk to him?' she asked Emmie.

'Yes, if he wants to talk to me...to say...whatever he needs...' Emmie faltered, feeling her heart flutter at the thought of talking to him. What would she say? What would he say?

Judith hurried through to the hallway, and Emmie heard the familiar deep voice pour through to the kitchen.

'I won't come in,' Hunter told Judith. 'But I'd like to have a word with Emmie.'

117

The excitement roared through her, the rush of adrenalin, as she hurried to the front door. She tried to appear calm, but seeing him standing there in the shaded sunlight pouring through the trees, caused her heart to jolt. He wore a light cream shirt and trousers several tones deeper, and looked the most handsome she'd ever seen him.

His heart reacted when he saw Emmie, so beautiful in her lovely dress and cute socks. Her pale grey eyes gazed at him, and he wasn't sure if he was welcome in her life or not.

Judith scurried away, leaving them to talk in private.

Seeing Emmie, he fought the urge to wrap her in his arms and squeeze the breath from her, so relieved that she was safe. But he kept his feelings hidden, and instead he said, 'Are you okay?'

She nodded calmly while inside she felt a tidal wave of emotion wash over her. Was she okay? Yes? No, not really. 'I'll be fine.' It was the nearest to the truth she could say.

'It must've been frightening being lost in the forest at night. Not that you were lost. You just kept not finding where you should be going.'

She smiled, remembering when they'd first met.

'I have no right to ask you to wait for me,' he began. 'And I'm not going to. But I will tell you that I have every intention of coming back.'

She absorbed his words. 'Good intentions and all that...' It wasn't meant as a rebuke.

'I plan to come back, Emmie. But I have to leave.'

'I understand. Movie deals don't happen every day.'

'That's true, but the meeting with the producers, the director, the investors...all of that will be dealt with. It may seem like I'm flying off to this new, glitzy, movie world, but when the meetings are over and the deals made, things will rattle back down to the same thing.'

She frowned at him.

'Me, sitting at my laptop, hammering away, writing the books and maybe helping to write the scripts.'

She pictured him sitting in his cottage working away, writing, and she started to understand.

'The glamour is fleeting. The real work is in the writing. I spend most of my time at home sitting writing. So if there's any chance that you think, as I do, that we could have a future together, then you should know that I'm going to be home a lot. Just not yet. I have to go make these deals.'

She wanted to promise that she'd wait for him, but past experiences made her unwilling to put her heart in jeopardy again. She nodded that she understood.

Her silence prompted him to tell her something else before he left. 'I won't call you. I'll give you time to yourself, to do what you would've done if I hadn't stepped into your world.' He smiled and then walked away to his car.

She fought back the tears that were threatening to make her look like a complete fool. She folded her arms across her chest, as if to hold her emotions tight as she let him walk away, perhaps forever.

As he reached his car he looked over his shoulder at her one last time and said, 'I'm coming back, Emmie.'

And then he got into his car and drove off quickly before he changed his mind and asked her to forgive him for everything, and tell her that he'd fallen in love with her. He'd fallen the first time he'd met her. And when it came right down to it, he'd loved her before that. The woman in his novels. He wrote about her and now she was in his life for real.

Emmie watched the sleek black sports car disappear into the forest. She blinked away the tears.

Hunter was gone.

Calum's training schedule became intense preparing for the forthcoming fight. Not long now. He'd be leaving soon. His training was fierce. Early morning runs through the forest, swimming along the coast, exercises, weights, shadow boxing in the postmaster's garden at night, hitting the punch bag until he punched it so hard he broke the chain that was holding it up.

He continued to cook dinner for the postmaster, and helped him when he was extra busy with parcels and deliveries for the couriers.

He thought about asking Emmie to have dinner with him. He'd told her that he'd cook for her. But Emmie was always busy working at the dressmaker's cottage, attending the sewing bee nights, or at home in the strawberry jam cottage designing her embroidery patterns.

When he ran through the forest every day, Judith waved to him a few times and invited him in for tea. He'd accepted each time, hoping to see Emmie, but she was always due to arrive later, at her own cottage or with Ethel.

But on the last morning he walked into the living room at the dressmaker's cottage, he heard someone using the sewing machine in the sewing room. He smiled, thinking it was Emmie, but it was Tiree.

'Tiree is the dressmaker's apprentice,' Judith explained while she poured Calum a cup of tea. 'She's been helping us again.'

'Emmie's coming up here later on,' the dressmaker told him, sensing he wondered why she wasn't there. 'She's updating her website with her new embroidery patterns.'

Calum nodded and drank his tea.

He enjoyed his visits, the ladies company, and they were happy to have Calum in their world.

They never mentioned Hunter, and he never asked.

'I'll be leaving soon,' he told them.

'We're all going to watch the fight,' said Judith. 'The postmaster says it's being televised on one of the sports channels. He's having a night of it at his house with his large screen telly. We're all going to have a wee party and cheer you on.'

'I appreciate the support from all of you,' he said, wishing he could confirm his plans would include coming back to the village. But nothing was settled and it wouldn't be until the fight was over.

'Tavion and I are having a party at his farmhouse tomorrow night,' Tiree told him. 'Come along if your training allows for it.'

'Tiree and Tavion have set a date for their wedding,' said the dressmaker.

Judith beamed. 'They're getting married in the autumn.'

'Congratulations,' Calum told Tiree.

'And Mairead and Fintry have set a date for their wedding,' said Judith. 'They didn't manage to get married last winter due to Fintry's flower hunting work. But Mairead is going to be a snow bride this winter.'

Calum nodded and smiled. Inside, he was wishing that a third wedding was scheduled. He would've married Emmie in a heartbeat.

'Cover your ears, Tiree,' Judith said jokingly. Then she revealed to Calum, 'The sewing bee are making two wedding ring quilts. An autumn theme one for Tiree, and a winter pattern one for Mairead.'

'They sound lovely,' he said.

After his tea, he got ready to leave, having promised he'd try his best to pop in to Tiree and Tavion's party the following night.

'There will be dancing,' Judith told him. 'Calum trained in dancing,' she said to Tiree.

'Will you be going to the party?' he asked the dressmaker.

'No, I'll be busy here,' the dressmaker said, smiling.

Judith and Tiree were used to the dressmaker not attending any of the local social events. They understood that she was happy in her cottage.

But Calum thought it was a shame, though he kept his thoughts to himself.

'I've always wanted to learn the tango,' Judith confessed.

'Wear your dancing shoes, Judith,' he said. 'And be prepared to tango with me.'

Judith clapped her hands with glee. 'Oh, wait until I tell Ethel and the other ladies.'

Calum left them to get on with their work, and continued his run through the forest. The summer was still hot. Some days he ran along the sand on the shore, but he liked the shade of the forest. The atmosphere of the forest was something he would miss when he left.

Emmie finished updating her website with her new embroidery patterns, and then drove up to work at the dressmaker's cottage until it was time for the sewing bee.

Tiree was busy getting things organised for the party the following night and didn't attend the sewing bee. Mairead was working on her botanical artwork at Fintry's cottage, and she wasn't there either.

The bee was busy with the ladies deciding what fabrics to use for the double wedding ring quilts. The autumn theme quilt for Tiree and Tavion would be easy because many of the members loved the autumn and had fabric scraps, from fat quarters to larger pieces, in autumnal tones of gold, bronze, copper, yellow and burnished colours that they were willing to contribute to create the quilt.

'The dressmaker gave me these pieces of fabric for your quilts.' Judith dug them out of her craft bag. 'She had these designs printed specially on to fabric for dresses she was making. There were plenty of pieces left, so here they are.' Judith unrolled the pieces and the women gathered to see what the prints were.

'This is perfect for Tiree,' Ethel exclaimed. She held up fabric that had been printed with little tea dresses.

Judith then showed them fabric the dressmaker had contributed for Mairead — beautiful vintage floral prints.

The ladies were delighted with these, and started to plan the wedding ring quilts.

Emmie joined in, keen to see their methods for creating the quilts and the tradition of making them for couples getting married in the local community.

'Are you into quilting, Emmie?' Hilda asked her.

'I've done a bit of quilting, small items, little patchworks and hexies for English paper piecing projects. But I've never made a larger quilt. I've seen double wedding ring quilts and they were gorgeous.'

'They're one of my favourite designs,' Hilda told her.

The chatter filled the room and teacups and spoons rattled as the kettle went on for tea.

A man's voice spoke up to make himself heard. 'Can I come in, ladies?'

Calum stood there holding two large white cakes boxes.

'Come in,' Ethel said, welcoming him to join them.

'I asked Cuan McVey for a couple of his chocolatier speciality cakes. Where can I put them down?'

Ethel cleared her yarn from a table. 'Put them down here, thank you.'

Calum sat them down and opened the lid on the top box to show them a large chocolate fudge cake decorated with chocolate buttercream and chocolate truffles. 'I thought the rum truffles would go well with your ginger wine, Ethel. The one with the extra raspberry essence.'

Ethel giggled. 'They certainly will.'

'I can't stay long as I'm going for a run,' Calum explained. 'But I wanted to say a proper goodbye to all of you, to thank you for your kindness and friendship. I'll see most of you at Tiree and Tavion's party tomorrow night, but I didn't want to spoil their happy celebration. So I'll say goodbye here.'

He hadn't anticipated the hugs he received, kisses on the cheek, and the warmth they wrapped him in before letting him go.

'Will you be coming back?' Ione asked him.

'I intend to,' he said without any firm date or further assurance.

The ladies didn't press him for this.

He glanced around him, smiled and said, 'Enjoy your cake and truffles. I'll see you at the party.'

All of the women nodded as they intended going to Tiree's party.

Emmie was the only one to remain still. She'd planned to join the dressmaker in her cottage to get on with an evening of sewing. So this was the last time she'd see Calum before he left to go home for ten days training at the boxing club to get ready for the fight event in London.

Calum glanced at Emmie, noticing she was the only one that didn't nod, but he saw no reason why she wouldn't be there. Things felt a little awkward between them. A feeling he didn't want. He thought the party would give him the chance to dance with her.

Ethel, Hilda, Bea, Ione and Aurora saw him out, waving and thanking him for the chocolatier's cakes.

Emmie thought about running after Calum and shouting, 'I hope you win.' But she hesitated too long. She heard him leave. Calum had gone. She wondered if she'd ever see him again.

'Would you like a slice of chocolate cake?' Ethel asked Emmie, as Hilda and two other ladies made the tea.

'Yes please,' Emmie said to her.

'Calum was looking extra fit tonight,' Aurora commented.

'He's been doing extra exercises and running through the forest every morning,' Judith told them.

Aurora nodded. 'It shows. He's extremely fit and strong.'

'Calum is a fine young man,' Judith said, sounding quite proud of him.

During the sewing bee, Emmie learned techniques to improve her quilting, and enjoyed watching the ladies make a start on the wedding ring quilts.

Later, Emmie walked back to her cottage having enjoyed a fun night at the sewing bee. But when she went inside the cottage, made a cup of tea, and got ready for bed, she felt all alone. This made her a bit teary, especially when she thought about Hunter...and Calum.

Nothing felt settled in Emmie's world. Nothing was.

Emmie helped the dressmaker work on two dresses the following morning. Tiree was getting things ready for the party, so she'd skipped popping up to help them.

Judith busied herself knitting and baking scones.

It was another scorching day. The patio doors were open to allow a warm breeze to waft in. Thimble lay stretched out on the lawn enjoying the warmth of the sunshine.

Instead of going home at dinner time, Emmie stayed and had something to eat with the dressmaker. They enjoyed the savoury casserole and minted new potatoes that Judith had cooked for dinner.

Afterwards, Judith cleared up the dishes, put her cardigan on, picked up her bag and smiled. 'Right, I'm away to get my glad rags on for the party. I'll see you two in the morning.' And off she went.

Emmie wasn't staying the night at the dressmaker's cottage, just a few hours to help finish the dresses they'd been working on during the day. There was a calm and comforting atmosphere in the cottage even when they were busy, and she loved the feeling of being in the heart of the forest, tucked away from the world.

'I'm on the promise of a dance,' said Calum, arriving at the party when it was at its height. He wore black trousers and a dark shirt, and had attempted to tame his unruly hair.

The guests looked round at him.

Judith put her hand up in the air. 'I put my dancing shoes on. Or at least a pair that I can jig in.'

Calum had lined up tango music on his phone. He sat it down and pressed play.

Judith started to giggle. 'I've never done the tango. It always looks so...'

'Sexy,' shouted Big Sam.

'Classy,' Judith said, smiling.

Calum seemed at ease taking Judith in hold and leading her into the dance.

The guests cheered as Calum led Judith and dipped her a few times.

Aurora helpfully filmed it. Something else for the archives and happy times shared.

Calum bowed and smiled at Judith when they finished dancing. 'That was great, Judith.'

'I'm enjoying doing things I wouldn't have thought I'd do.' She smiled at Calum. 'It's your influence young man. Encouraging me to run in the three-legged race and now dance the tango.'

'When's your fight?' Tavion asked him.

'Ten days from now. I'm leaving tonight.'

Ethel and the others overhead him.

Calum shrugged his broad shoulders. 'I have to go. It's better to drive through the night. I wouldn't sleep for thinking anyway. I'm so focussed on the fight.'

They understood.

'You're coming back though?' Ethel said to him.

'I will. I'll come for a visit,' Calum promised.

He thanked them again for everything, and then hurried away before he caused any more interruption to the happy couple's party.

'My house is going to feel empty without Calum,' the postmaster said to Ethel.

She nodded and looked over at Judith, chatting to some of the party guests, buzzing that she'd danced the tango, and telling them that she'd put the trophy she'd won in her display cabinet.

'Calum's been a good influence on Judith, and I suspect the dressmaker too,' said Ethel.

'The dressmaker made him welcome in her cottage. She doesn't usually encourage too many visitors. But I've noticed that she's been more...'

'Sociable?' Ethel suggested.

The postmaster nodded.

Ione came bounding up to them. 'We're going to dance a fast–moving reel, so come on. You two can link up with Big Sam and me.'

Grabbing Ethel's hand, Ione pulled them into the ceilidh dancing that continued well into the night.

Tavion's farmhouse was aglow with lights, music, laughter and dancing as Emmie drove past his flower field on her way home from the dressmaker's cottage. She pictured the lively party, but she was glad she'd chosen to help the dressmaker with the sewing. It was a calmer evening, and she'd enjoyed sitting in the sewing room chatting while they made the dresses for the television series. Sometimes, when she thought about it, a rush of excitement went through her, realising that the dresses she was helping to stitch and embroider were going to be worn for audiences to see.

She continued to drive past the farmhouse down to her cottage on the shore. There would be other parties, but she was happy learning so many techniques and tips from working with the dressmaker.

She parked her car outside her cottage, gazed out over the calm sea glistening under the night sky, breathed in the fresh air, and then went inside to get some sleep.

In the distance, further up near the fields, the tail lights of Calum's silver grey car faded into the night. He'd hoped that Emmie would've been at Tiree and Tavion's party so that he could say goodbye and maybe dance with her. Perhaps another time. Bottling up his disappointment, he continued driving away heading back home to the city.

CHAPTER TWELVE

By the Sea

Over the next week, Emmie concentrated on working at the dressmaker's cottage during the day and sometimes stayed to have dinner and continued sewing at night, finishing the embroidery.

Ethel invited her to have dinner one evening, and she learned how to spin the yarn, and stitched part of the wedding ring quilts for Mairead and Tiree at the sewing bee night.

Working with the dressmaker, she enjoyed what she'd come there for, a break away from the city, not a broken heart or the hopes of a romance. But there was something missing. One night, driving back down after finishing work for the day, she realised what it was. When she saw Hunter's cottage cast in shadows, empty, she knew that something, someone, was Hunter.

After a busy day working with the dressmaker, and an evening of embroidery in her cottage, Emmie made herself a cup of tea and sipped it sitting at the kitchen table. The kitchen door was open and the warm night air wafted in. She wore a pretty cotton tea dress and her hair hung silky smooth around her shoulders. The fragrance of the garden's night scented stock flowers, roses and jasmine, merged with the strawberry jam scent that lingered in the kitchen, especially on warm summer evenings.

She liked living in the cottage, but she'd hadn't quite settled in it. Perhaps it was because nothing in her life was settled, and that included her relationship with Hunter. She wondered if she'd see him again or if he'd forgotten about her.

A knock on the front door jolted her from her thoughts. She peered through the living room window and gasped when she saw the black sports car parked outside.

She hurried to open the door, and there was Hunter standing gazing at her, looking so tall and handsome.

'Hunter!' Her heart thundered and she could hardly believe that he was there. It was after midnight.

'Can I come in?'

'Yes, I...I didn't expect to see you...' the surprise shook her to the core, and she heard herself falter.

He stepped inside and closed the door. 'I promised I'd come back.'

She nodded, gazing into those beautiful blue eyes of his, fighting back the urge to throw her arms around him and tell him that she'd missed him so much. But there was something in his expression that made her hesitate.

'I can't stay long,' he said.

Emmie's heart clenched. The disappointment hit her hard. He'd only just arrived, and now he couldn't stay.

'The meetings in London went well. I got the movie deal. But now I have to fly to New York to meet with producers and investors there. It's part of the deal. I have to go.'

Emmie nodded, trying to hide her disappointment behind a resigned smile. 'I understand. I hope you find success there.'

He gazed down at her. 'But I wanted to ask you...to come with me.'

Emmie blinked. 'To New York?'

'Yes, we'd have to leave tonight, now, as soon as you're packed.'

The feelings his offer created sent her senses reeling. Was she hearing right? It had been a long, tiring day.

Hunter stepped closer. 'Come with me, Emmie.'

She hesitated. 'I can't just leave,' she managed to say.

'Why not?'

'Because...' her mind felt befuddled as she searched for the first reason.

'The only thing that's holding you here is your work with the dressmaker,' he said.

This was true — and that's when she remembered what the dressmaker had told her. 'Make the decisions that suit you,' she'd advised Emmie. And then emphasised, 'Don't miss out on any chances you're offered because you feel you're letting me down.'

At the time she hadn't understood, but now it made sense. She told Hunter.

'Then hurry up. Let's go.'

'It's too late to phone the dressmaker,' Emmie said as she threw her things in a couple of cases. 'I'll call her in the morning and explain what's happened.'

Hunter helped Emmie pack. 'Anything else you need, we'll buy when we get to New York. And leave your car here. We'll deal with that later.'

Emmie checked the cottage one last time while Hunter put her cases in the car. She intended coming back. But would she? This felt like the last night she'd be here.

'Come on, Emmie,' Hunter called to her.

She flicked the lights off, closed the front door, and got into the car.

The moment she sat down, she felt like she had before, that sense of what life would be like if she was with Hunter in his world. And here she was, about to leave this piece of her past behind, and fly off with him to New York. She'd never done anything so impulsive, so daring and adventurous. But maybe, just maybe, it was time to throw caution to the wind and live a little, live a lot.

Hunter drove off. There was no one around to see them leave. The esplanade was quiet. Everyone was at home, asleep in bed.

The sense of excitement made Emmie smile over at Hunter. He smiled back at her.

She glanced one last time out the car window at the shimmering sea in the distance, and then looked ahead as Hunter drove them away from the shore and the forest, heading to the city, to the airport, to catch their flight to New York.

The next morning Judith walked into the dressmaker's cottage and heard the dressmaker's light laughter as she chatted to someone on the phone.

They nodded acknowledgment. Judith put her knitting bag down and went into the kitchen to make their morning tea. She'd brought fresh bread, rolls and scones with her.

'I'm delighted for you, Emmie. Yes, of course you should've gone. Don't worry about things here. You've worked hard and helped me finish so many of the dresses. You've barely had any time for yourself. I couldn't have asked for more from you.'

Judith popped her head out of the kitchen on hearing Emmie's name.

The dressmaker continued her call. 'I wish you every happiness in New York, Emmie.'

Judith's gasped and mouthed — *New York*?

'Yes, do keep in touch and let us know how you're getting on.'

Clicking the phone off, the dressmaker smiled at Judith. 'Emmie's gone. She left after midnight last night with Hunter.'

'Hunter?'

'He drove here to ask her to go with him to New York. He got his movie deal, but now he has to meet more film people in New York,' the dressmaker explained. 'Emmie left here to go with him to the city, to the airport.'

Judith plopped down on a chair. 'How long will she be away? Is she coming back?'

The dressmaker shrugged. 'She doesn't know. It depends on Hunter's deals. But she did say that once the deals are done, he has to come home to finish writing the last novel in the series. He's on a deadline now with it. His agent and publishers want him to finish it so they can start promoting it as part of the movie deal.'

'It's all very exciting.' Judith's heart was racing. 'Does anyone else here know?'

'No, she's asked us to explain to Ethel, the sewing bee ladies, everyone.'

The kettle started to boil. Judith stood up and went through to make the tea.

They sat at the kitchen table drinking their tea and chatting.

'I'll pop down to the strawberry jam cottage later and clear any food that's in the fridge or cupboards,' said Judith.

'Emmie left the keys to the cottage and her car keys on the hall table. Hunter's arranging for someone to come and pick her car up and drive it to his house in the city.'

'It definitely doesn't sound as if Emmie's coming back any time soon, if ever.'

'We have to remember, she's a city girl. She never really seemed to settle here.'

'Hunter and Calum may have had something to do with that.'

The dressmaker agreed. 'But she deserves to find love and happiness with the right man.'

'I will miss her, but I do wish her every happiness.'

'So do I, Judith.'

Judith poured more tea. 'Tiree says she'll be here later. She's helping to tidy up Tavion's farmhouse after the party.' She paused and reflected. 'It'll be you, me and Tiree again working in the sewing room. The way it used to be.'

The dressmaker nodded and sipped her tea while Judith phoned Ethel to tell her the news about Emmie and Hunter. Ethel told the postmaster and Aurora, and soon everyone knew.

The day was a scorcher, but the dressmaker worked on her designs in the sewing room, determined to get a lot of work done.

Tiree arrived after lunch and helped with the sewing. While they worked they chatted about Emmie and Hunter, and Judith dancing with Calum at the party the previous night.

Judith made ice cream and lemonade drinks for the three of them for their afternoon tea, and Thimble snoozed in the sunshine.

Their lives would've settled into enjoying the summer, but soon there was talk of Calum's impending fight. The postmaster organised the party at his house on the evening of the event.

Guests arrived an hour ahead of the event to enjoy the run up to the contest, discussing Calum's opponent, the clear favourite to win.

'I'm still backing Calum,' the postmaster announced as they watched and listened to the large screen television in his spacious living room. Everyone in their circle of friends was there, except the dressmaker. She was at home in her cottage.

'Have you spoken to Calum recently?' Aurora asked the postmaster.

'Yes, I spoke to him a couple of days ago,' the postmaster told her. 'He knows he's got a tough opponent, but he's intending fighting like a tiger for the title.'

'Does he know about Emmie and Hunter?' Hilda asked him.

'Nooo, he asked me about her, as he always does when he phones, but I didn't tell him she'd left and gone away with Hunter. I didn't want to upset him before his fight,' the postmaster explained.

The dressmaker's sewing machine whirred in the quiet cottage as she stitched a satin dress.

She checked the time, intending to watch Calum's fight on the television. Almost time to make herself a cup of tea and settle down in the living room to enjoy the contest.

Her phone rang as she finished sewing the hem. She picked up and smiled when she heard the familiar voice.

'I hope I'm not disturbing you,' Calum began, 'but I wondered if Emmie was there. She's been working a lot of nights with you. I wanted to talk to her for a minute. I'm due to fight. This is the last phone call before I put the gloves on.'

'Emmie's not here, Calum. She left a few days ago. She's gone to New York with Hunter.'

The news hit him harder than any punch he'd sustain in his forthcoming bout.

The dressmaker hoped she'd done the right thing telling him.

'Thanks for telling me. I'll see you when I come back. Thanks again for everything.' He was gone before she could wish him well for his fight, but she sensed he knew this.

She made her tea and settled down in the living room to watch the match unfold.

A cheer erupted in the postmaster's house as they watched the television. Calum appeared, looking fighting fit and strong, and walked through the audience towards the ring.

Ethel smiled with glee. 'He's wearing the robe we made for him.'

'It suits him,' said Hilda.

'He looks very fit,' Ione added.

'And angry, like he's ready for a fight,' said Aurora.

The postmaster agreed. 'I've never seen him look so...ferocious. He must've worked himself up, getting set to take on his opponent.'

Tavion put his arm around Tiree as they sat together. 'I haven't seen any of his fights, but he's got an intense look to him. I wouldn't like to take him on.'

'Come on, Calum!' Ethel cheered him on as he climbed into the ring. Lit up under the glaring lights, he took off his robe to reveal his fit body. He punched his gloves together as the fight was seconds away from starting.

The postmaster leaned forward to study Calum's face. 'He's definitely got an angry look to him. I hope no one has said anything to upset him before his fight.'

The dressmaker saw the intense look on his face too. She wished him all the luck, as the fight started.

The postmaster and the others cheered throughout the first three minute round. Calum was on the attack, and the favourite had to defend himself stronger than he'd anticipated.

They jumped up and clapped in the third round as the fight ended with a knockout from Calum.

'He won!' the postmaster shouted. 'Calum won!'

The dressmaker sat on her own, but cheered when Calum won the title.

She smiled and watched him being presented with the winner's trophy. He held it aloft. With the fight being over in the third round and Calum's tenacious fighting, he'd barely endured a hit.

Flicking the television off, she went into the sewing room and continued to finish one of the dresses.

Thimble came padding in from outside and settled in his cosy bed.

Judith phoned. 'Did you watch the fight?'

'I did. I'm delighted Calum won.'

'Did you see the ferocious look on his face?'

'Yes. He phoned me just before the contest,' the dressmaker told her.

Judith paused. 'What did you say to him?'

She told her.

'No wonder he looked upset.'

Hunter had booked a table in one of the top restaurants in New York. They had a wonderful view of the city at night.

'Look at all the lights,' Emmie said, gazing out at the view.

Hunter admired the view. But not the lights of New York. Sitting across the table from Emmie as they enjoyed dinner, he thought that she looked beautiful. She radiated happiness. He hoped they'd get along. They'd both taken a chance that their relationship would flourish away from the constrains of their regular lives. Flying to New York was an adventure they shared.

They stayed in adjoining rooms in a plush hotel organised by the film company. Instead of Emmie feeling that she wasn't part of

Hunter's world, she was included at the dinners and parties he needed to attend. He'd told them that he'd met her and she was the woman he'd described years ago when he'd written the first novel in the series. They loved this idea and thought it could become part of the marketing. She'd packed her embroidery in her craft bag and brought it with her thinking she could work on her patterns while Hunter was busy. Tucked into her bag were hexies for an English paper piecing project the sewing bee ladies had encouraged her to try — a mini quilt. Ethel's yarn samples were also included for knitting. But amid the whirlwind of excitement with Hunter she'd been too busy to do any of these.

As for being a couple, they became closer each day, though they slept in separate adjoining rooms, to begin with. Hunter didn't want to pressure Emmie, even though the fire and love and longing for her was overwhelming. He wanted the timing to be right for both of them.

'New York is everything I dreamed it would be,' Emmie said, gazing out at the city and then smiling at Hunter.

He lifted his glass of wine in a toast. 'To you and me, Emmie.'

'To us,' she said, and sipped her wine.

'We've a busy day tomorrow,' he told her as they started to eat their dinner. He'd ordered chicken and fresh vegetables.

Emmie opted for a delicious pasta dish and crisp green salad. And tea.

'I thought we should go back to the hotel after dinner. Have an early night. I know we spoke about taking in a show—'

'We're here for at least another week before we fly home to Scotland,' she said. 'Let's have an early night.'

The intense look he gave her sent her senses wild. She knew that look. Was it time to take their relationship to the next level?

'I don't want to rush you, to put pressure on you,' he insisted.

Her smile reassured him that she wanted to be closer to him.

He leaned over and kissed her gently. 'Are you sure you think this is a sensible idea?'

'No, I think it's impulsive, exciting and throw a hint of danger into the mix.'

'Danger?'

The look she gave him melted his heart. In danger of falling in love with him. Hard. For ever.

'I won't ever break your heart, Emmie.' His words rang true and strong.

She nodded. She believed him.

For the first time, they snuggled up in Hunter's bed and enjoyed a loving and intimate night together.

'I should warn you that I have no intention of ever letting you go,' he murmured to her, wrapping her in his loving arms, holding her close.

'Warning accepted.' She snuggled into him, and fell asleep.

The meeting the next day was a success, and a further movie deal was agreed.

During their trip to New York, Hunter managed to continue writing his book, feeling inspired by the Big Apple and all the excitement of the city that never seemed to sleep.

One evening late at night, Emmie wandered through from her bedroom to where Hunter was sitting typing by the glow of his laptop. Behind him, the hotel bedroom suite's main window gave a view of the glittering lights of New York.

She wrapped her arms around his neck from behind and gave him a kiss on the cheek.

'Feeling inspired?' she asked, becoming accustomed to the fast typing when the story flowed from his fingertips.

He typed a final word, pressed save, and smiled at her. 'I've just written the ending. The last chapter of the last book in this series.'

'You've finished writing your novel?'

He stood up and eased the hours of tension from his shoulders, sitting at his laptop writing late at night. 'No, I've written a lot, but I've sort of blocked in the storyline for the last couple of chapters. I want the ending nailed before I add more details to the remainder of the story.'

'I hope you've written a happy ending for your heroine this time,' she said, smiling at him.

He nodded firmly. 'I have.'

'Are you allowed to tell me what happens or is the ending a secret?'

'It's not a secret from you.'

She listened while he told her the ending.

135

'The hero asks her to marry him.'

'What does she say?'

'She says yes.'

'And they live happily every after I suppose?'

'That's the plan.' He pulled her into his arms and pressed his firm lips against hers, kissing her with all the passion she'd come to expect and long for from Hunter.

'I love that plan,' she said softly.

'And I love you, Emmie. I think we'll have a great life together.'

Emmie nodded. 'I think so too.' As he pulled her close she smiled. 'I love you, Hunter.'

She felt his embrace strengthen as he held her close. 'I love you too, Emmie.'

They stood together gazing out at the lights of New York.

Wrapped safely in his arms she looked at the glittering city. 'What happens now?'

'We've a few more days of meetings in New York, and then we'll fly home to Scotland.' He paused. 'I thought you'd like to come home with me, to my house, in the city.'

Her heart thundered with excitement. 'Yes, I'd like that.'

'And from there, well...I have to finish the book, become part of the movie deal plans, so we'd be living in the city until we decided where we wanted to settle down.'

Emmie snuggled into Hunter, feeling happy and content for the first time in a long while, finally knowing in her heart that she was with the man she was meant to be with.

She wondered if the dressmaker knew, or sensed that this was the best gift she could ever have given to her. The dressmaker had asked her to bring the vintage dresses to her cottage, and in doing so she met Hunter. Was that the dressmaker's gift to her? Happiness with Hunter? She suspected she'd never know, but she preferred to think that the dressmaker was a bit fey, intuitive. Gazing out at New York, Emmie wished the dressmaker well and hoped she'd enjoy more happiness in her life too.

'Come on, let's get some sleep. An early start in the morning and a busy day ahead.' Hunter took her hand and led her through to her bedroom.

'Sleep?' Emmie giggled.

Hunter laughed, lifted her up in his arms and carried her through, with no intention of getting much sleep.

Judith came bustling into the dressmaker's cottage carrying a bag of groceries and her knitting bag. 'Morning. It's going to be another scorcher. The sun's streaming through the forest.' She put her knitting bag down and hurried through to the kitchen and started unpacking the groceries. 'I'm a wee bit late, but I was nattering to Ethel and Aurora. The magazine's boosted the sales of Ethel's new yarn, and Hilda's had orders for her quilts. I was reading my copy last night on my laptop. It's the best issue I've read. It gets better every month. Have you read any of it yet?'

'Not yet, but I will.' The dressmaker was selecting fabric from the shelves in the living room and they chatted while working.

'The pictures of your original dresses are beautiful, and your fashion illustrations look perfect,' said Judith. 'Aurora added Calum's win to his feature, and she says that loads of people are entering the competitions to win the knitted items and a signed copy of Hunter's book.'

'I'll look forward to reading the magazine later.'

'I've lots of news to tell you,' Judith continued while filling the kettle for tea. 'Emmie sent a wee message saying she's still in New York with Hunter — and he's been hinting about buying her a ring.'

'Another engagement soon then.'

'Oh, I think so.' She paused. 'Tiree asked me not to tell you, but she's in a tizzy trying to make her wedding dress.'

'Tiree is a very capable seamstress. What's wrong?'

'She's so excited about getting married soon, and isn't sure what fabric to use, or if the dress she has in mind would suit her. She doesn't want to ask you because you're busy making the dresses for the television series.'

'I'm almost done. I finished those two last night.' The dressmaker indicated to the dresses on the mannequins.

Judith peered round and gasped. 'Those are gorgeous.'

'I'll have everything finished in a couple of days. Tell Tiree to bring her dress here to me. Or the design she's planning.'

Judith smiled. 'Thank you. I think she's just too excited.'

'I'll even make her dress for her.'

Judith clapped her hands. 'That would be wonderful.'

The dressmaker selected a bolt of blue satin from the shelf and held it up to the light shining in through the patio doors. The sapphire blue would be perfect for the cocktail dress she was due to make.

'I met the postmaster when I was buying my shopping,' Judith said, setting up the tea cups. 'He says that Calum has finished doing the rounds of publicity, the interviews, after his win. He has another fight soon, but he's popping back for a quick visit to see us.'

'When's he due back?'

'Later today I think. I'm looking forward to seeing him.'

The dressmaker nodded. 'Yes, so am I.'

'The postmaster also said he's heard that Bramble cottage is going to be up for sale in the autumn. And one of the shops down the shore is moving away to open up in the city. So, it's all go at the moment.' Judith poured their tea and buttered their fruit scones.

The dressmaker had news too. 'The film company I designed dresses for—'

'The one where we attended the film premiere in London?' Judith clarified.

'Yes. They phoned me last night. It was quite late or I'd have called to tell you, but with the time difference in Hollywood, I thought you'd be asleep.'

'Hollywood phoned you?'

'They've asked me to design the dresses for another film.'

'Have you accepted?' Judith sounded hopeful. She loved the excitement of being involved in the outskirts of Hollywood. Maybe they'd be invited to attend the London premiere of that movie.

'Yes, but they want me to fly out to Hollywood to meet the stars.'

Judith didn't expect the dressmaker to have agreed to that part of the deal. London was a big enough deal the last time.

'I've been thinking lately that I should...live a little more...' the dressmaker began.

Judith knew that tone. 'You've agreed to fly to Hollywood?'

The dressmaker nodded.

'When do you leave?'

'Next week. They want me to attend dinners, parties, meet the stars. I'll be designing the dresses for the main scenes with their leading lady, Charmaine Charlatain. The two male leads are Shaw Starlight and Bradley Goldsilver.'

Judith gasped. 'Bradley Goldsilver! He's my heartthrob.'

'I'll come back here to design the dresses, but I have to fly out to Hollywood to meet them.'

'How long will you be away?'

'We'll be away for two weeks.'

Judith blinked. 'We?'

'I thought you'd like to go with me.'

Judith smiled. 'To Hollywood? Oh, yes, I'd love to.'

'We'll fly to New York, but instead of catching a connecting flight to Los Angeles, I thought we could enjoy a couple of days shopping there.'

'Shopping in New York?' Judith sounded so excited.

'Then we'll fly to LA.'

Judith couldn't stand still for the excitement. She ran around the living room cheering. 'This is wonderful. I'm so excited.'

'I'll ask Ethel to look after Thimble,' said the dressmaker. 'You know how he loves the yarn in Ethel's cottage.'

'She'll make him woolly pom poms like the last time she watched him when we went to London. He'll be spoiled rotten.'

'That's Thimble's holidays sorted.'

Judith was still bouncing with joy.

The dressmaker's smile faded for a moment. 'There's only one thing...'

Judith frowned. 'What?'

The dressmaker went over to the walk–in cupboard filled with rails of beautiful dresses and opened the doors. 'What are we going to wear?'

They both started laughing.

The dressmaker lifted a dazzling red cocktail dress and held it up. 'I think this one has your name on it. There was plenty of that gorgeous fabric left so I made another one.'

Judith accepted the dress. 'I'll wear this, if you wear the gold one.'

The dressmaker selected a shimmering gold evening dress and held it up. The chiffon hem was embroidered with gold beads and it was a classy mid–length design.

Buzzing with excitement they stepped into the cupboard and began browsing for all the dresses they'd wear in Hollywood.

Thimble snoozed happily outside in the garden, enjoying the sunshine, while their laughter filled the air.

Ethel managed to parcel up her extra orders of yarn and take them to the post office in time for the courier collection. She waited and chatted to the postmaster while he cleared everything and closed up.

The early evening sun shone a mellow gold through the post office windows. It was a lovely summer night.

'I've just one thing to do before we lock up,' the postmaster said, remembering the small poster a young woman had sent, asking if it could be pinned up on the notice board. She'd photocopied a picture of herself and given details that she was looking for accommodation during the autumn.

He pinned it up. 'She seems like a lovely young woman.'

Ethel peered at the notice. 'She's very pretty. What is it she wants?'

'Local accommodation for the autumn. She says she's a baker.'

'The farmhouses will have vacancies by then, after the summer holidaymakers have gone,' said Ethel. 'I wonder what she's planning to do here in the autumn?'

The postmaster shrugged. 'Bake cakes?'

Flicking off the lights, they went outside and he locked the post office for the evening.

Ethel gazed out at the sea. The esplanade was quiet. Barely anyone except... She blinked. 'Am I seeing things?'

'What is it?' He looked in the direction of the laughter and voices chattering in the distance far along the shore, down on the sand, silhouetted against the shimmering sea.

'Is that Calum with Judith...and the dressmaker?' said Ethel.

'It is!' the postmaster exclaimed. 'Calum must have encouraged the dressmaker to enjoy herself down the shore.'

Ethel went to hurry away to join them, but the postmaster said, 'No, Ethel. Let them enjoy their time by themselves. It's progress that the dressmaker is there. Maybe she'll start joining in the sewing bee at your cottage.'

Ethel's eyes flickered with excitement. 'Wouldn't that be wonderful.' She watched them for a moment. 'Calum has been a great influence on her, and on Judith.'

The postmaster nodded and smiled warmly.

Ethel went to walk away home to her cottage.

'Would you like to come home with me for a wee bit of dinner?' he offered. 'We could watch a film on the telly.'

Ethel hesitated. 'I've a lot of yarn to spin for more orders.'

The postmaster smiled and nodded. He was used to her always having reasons for not wanting to be with him. He started to walk away.

Ethel glanced at the dressmaker, then changed her mind and hurried after the postmaster. She linked her arm through his and they fell into an easy and comfortable step with each other.

'What film are we going to watch?' Ethel asked him.

He smiled warmly. 'Whatever one you want, Ethel. Whatever you want.'

While Judith decided to venture into the water for a paddle, Calum took a moment to ask the dressmaker something. He kept his tone low.

'Do you think Emmie will marry Hunter?' he said.

The dressmaker nodded.

It didn't come as a surprise, but the disappointment cut him deep anyway. He gazed out at the sea, his handsome face highlighted against the glittering water.

'There will be someone, a lovely young woman, for you, Calum. I'm sure of it.'

His green eyes glanced at her.

'You should come back here in the autumn.' The dressmaker emphasised this.

'The autumn?' he said.

'Yes, that would be a great time for you to come back here.' The reassurance in her voice made him thoughtful. He had no firm plans for the autumn. Continue training. Hope to eventually leave the boxing behind, part of his past, and start up his own restaurant here. Find a cottage.

Judith came running over to them giggling. 'The sea's warm. You should go for a paddle,' she encouraged the dressmaker.

141

Calum nodded. 'Come on, shoes off, and go for a paddle in the sea.'

'It's been a long time since I've been near the sea,' the dressmaker told him.

He smiled at her.

Stepping out of her summer pumps, the dressmaker walked over to the edge of the sea...and waded in. She smiled at Calum and Judith, enjoying the feeling of the sea and the view along the coast and out to the islands. This is how she remembered it.

Thimble sat on the sea wall watching them laughing and having fun.

Calum picked Judith up and swung her over the water, playfully threatening to throw her in. She knew he wouldn't, but she screamed anyway and giggled.

Thimble jumped down from the esplanade and padded across the sand to join them.

Their laughter and chatter filled the warm night air with happiness and hope.

In his heart Calum made a promise to himself. He'd come back in the autumn.

End

Embroidery Pattern

An embroidery pattern of The Dressmaker's Cottage, based on the book cover, is included here. It was designed by the author, De-ann Black.

You can download a printable version of the pattern from:
De-annBlack.com/CottagePattern

The pattern is also printed to scale on page 145 with instructions on pages 148.

The Dressmaker's Cottage Embroidery Pattern Instructions

Thread: use one or two strands of embroidery floss.

This design was sewn on white cotton fabric.

Hoop size: seven inches.

Trace the pattern on to the fabric.

Stitch the cottage roof, main outline, windows, curtains and door.
Then stitch the greenery and flowers.

Roof
Light grey — stem stitch.

Walls
Warm grey — outline stitch.

Windows
Warm grey — stem stitch.

Curtains
Pink — back stitch.
Blue — back stitch.

Door
Light grey - stem stitch & French knot.

Greenery
Light green - back stitch & single stitch.

Flowers
Mid blue, pale blue, pink, lilac and yellow.
Lazy daisy stitch (petals)
French knots (flower centres & flower scatter).
Single stitch

About the Author:

De-ann Black is a bestselling author, scriptwriter and former newspaper journalist. She has over 80 books published. Romance, crime thrillers, espionage novels, action adventure. And children's books (non-fiction rocket science books and children's fiction). She became an Amazon All-Star author in 2014 and 2015.

She previously worked as a full-time newspaper journalist for several years. She had her own weekly columns in the press. This included being a motoring correspondent where she got to test drive cars every week for the press for three years.

Before being asked to work for the press, De-ann worked in magazine editorial writing everything from fashion features to social news. She was the marketing editor of a glossy magazine. She is also a professional artist and illustrator. Fabric design, dressmaking, sewing, knitting and fashion are part of her work.

Additionally, De-ann has always been interested in fitness, and was a fitness and bodybuilding champion, 100 metre runner and mountaineer. As a former N.A.B.B.A. Miss Scotland, she had a weekly fitness show on the radio that ran for over three years.

De-ann trained in Shukokai karate, boxing, kickboxing, Dayan Qigong and Jiu Jitsu. She is currently based in Scotland.
Her colouring books and embroidery design books are available in paperback. These include Floral Nature Embroidery Designs and Scottish Garden Embroidery Designs.

Also by De-ann Black (Romance, Action/Thrillers & Children's books). See her Amazon Author page or website for further details about her books, screenplays, illustrations, art and fabric designs.
www.De-annBlack.com

Romance books:

Cottages, Cakes & Crafts series:
1. The Flower Hunter's Cottage
2. The Sewing Bee by the Sea
3. The Beemaster's Cottage
4. The Chocolatier's Cottage
5. The Bookshop by the Seaside
6. The Dressmaker's Cottage

Sewing, Crafts & Quilting series:
1. The Sewing Bee
2. The Sewing Shop

Quilting Bee & Tea Shop series:
1. The Quilting Bee
2. The Tea Shop by the Sea
3. Embroidery Cottage

Heather Park: Regency Romance

Snow Bells Haven series:
1. Snow Bells Christmas
2. Snow Bells Wedding

Summer Sewing Bee
Christmas Cake Chateau

Sewing, Knitting & Baking series:
1. The Tea Shop
2. The Sewing Bee & Afternoon Tea
3. The Christmas Knitting Bee
4. Champagne Chic Lemonade Money
5. The Vintage Sewing & Knitting Bee

The Tea Shop & Tearoom series:
1. The Christmas Tea Shop & Bakery
2. The Christmas Chocolatier
3. The Chocolate Cake Shop in New York at Christmas
4. The Bakery by the Seaside
5. Shed in the City

Tea Dress Shop series:
1. The Tea Dress Shop At Christmas
2. The Fairytale Tea Dress Shop In Edinburgh
3. The Vintage Tea Dress Shop In Summer

Christmas Romance series:
1. Christmas Romance in Paris
2. Christmas Romance in Scotland

Romance, Humour, Mischief series:
1. Oops! I'm the Paparazzi
2. Oops! I'm A Hollywood Agent
3. Oops! I'm A Secret Agent
4. Oops! I'm Up To Mischief

The Bitch-Proof Suit series:
1. The Bitch-Proof Suit
2. The Bitch-Proof Romance
3. The Bitch-Proof Bride

The Cure For Love
Dublin Girl
Why Are All The Good Guys Total Monsters?
I'm Holding Out For A Vampire Boyfriend

Action/Thriller books:
Love Him Forever
Someone Worse
Electric Shadows
The Strife Of Riley
Shadows Of Murder
Cast a Dark Shadow

Colouring books:
Flower Nature
Summer Garden
Spring Garden
Autumn Garden
Sea Dream
Festive Christmas
Christmas Garden
Christmas Theme
Flower Bee
Wild Garden
Faerie Garden Spring
Flower Hunter
Stargazer Space
Bee Garden
Scottish Garden Seasons

Embroidery Design books:
Floral Garden Embroidery Patterns
Floral Spring Embroidery Patterns
Christmas & Winter Embroidery Patterns
Floral Nature Embroidery Designs
Scottish Garden Embroidery Designs

Printed in Great Britain
by Amazon

82935867R00092